Seducing SERENITY

The Kontakt Series, Book 1

Katie Mettner

Katie Mettner

Seducing Serenity

Copyright 2020 Katie Mettner
All rights reserved for this book its content, including the cover art by Forward Authority Design. Except as permitted under the U.S. Copyright Act of 1976, no part of this publication may be reproduced, distributed, or transmitted in any form or by any means, or stored in a database or retrieval system, without prior permission of the publisher. The characters and events in this book are fictitious. Names, characters, and plots are a product of the author's imagination. Any similarity to real persons, living or dead, is coincidental and not intended by the author.

Katie Mettner

One

Serenity

The parking lot was empty other than a forest green Porsche convertible sitting near the door. Nothing says *I'm rich, powerful, and German* like a Porsche 911. My beat-up, hand-me-down, almost dead Buick stuck out like a sore thumb parked next to it. It was a serious case of beauty and the beast. When I walked past, I noticed the license plate on the Porsche read *Kontakt*. I smacked myself lightly on the forehead. No wonder I couldn't get a hit when I Googled it. Of course they'd use the German spelling. In my defense, I had only been given an hour to change my clothes and make the forty-minute drive here.

I didn't have time to do my due diligence. Standing here now, staring at the eerily empty parking lot, I wish I had.

The building before me was towering steel and glass that went on for miles. The steel made it intimidating while the windows welcomed you. Ironically, that was something often said of the German people themselves. I grasped the opaque door handle, and my eyes took in the European font etched into the glass door. One word. *Kontakt*. Wait? Does he own the whole building? I shook my head no. That wasn't possible. When I walked in, and the shine of the marble floor nearly blinded me, I was sure that wasn't possible. You'd have to be a billionaire to own an entire ten-story building, especially one this opulent. I glanced around the rest of the reception area where a cherry wood desk sat, sans receptionist. I wasn't going to get much help there.

"No place to go but up," I muttered after the elevator doors opened. I was suddenly nervous about more than just the job interview. My finger hovered over the elevator buttons. What floor? It would have been nice if my professor had given me more to go on here. A fissure of fear ran down my spine. I retreated from the elevators and paced a few steps in each direction, completely unsure what my next move should be. I'd taken a lot of risks in my life, some far more dangerous than walking into an unoccupied office building to meet an unknown man, but I couldn't say this wasn't dangerous. Regardless, I needed this job. I wanted this job. Hell, I wanted any job. I wanted to move out of the professor's house and get a place of my own, which was something I'd never had. Unless you counted that one time when I pitched a tent behind campus.

I noticed a building directory to the side of the elevator, not surprised when only one floor had a name next to it. "Kontakt Corporate occupies the ninth floor. Looks like Mr. Lars Jäger has almost made it to the top." I snickered when the doors to the elevator slid closed and lifted me upward.

Smoothing the jacket of my pantsuit down, I took a couple of deep, calming breaths. I had no idea what Lars was looking for in an applicant for this marketing position. With so little to go on, I hadn't bothered to bring anything with me other than my resume, a notepad, and a pen. Oh, and my pepper spray. You don't grow up the way I did and walk into an unknown situation completely unprepared. I wasn't dying to die today.

The doors opened, and I stepped out onto a rug done in muted browns and greys. It screamed high class, something I only knew about from my years of cleaning high-rise office buildings for the upper echelon of Miami during college. The reception area directly off the elevator was just as empty as the one downstairs. Apparently, no one had breathed life into the place yet.

"Hello?" I called out. "Mr. Jäger? Is anyone here?"

A disembodied voice answered me from the left and down the hallway. "In my office, Miss Matthews."

I rolled my eyes at his welcoming ways. "What if I'm not Miss Matthews?"

"You drive a Buick, white with red trim," he called back. "I noticed it in the parking lot."

"How did you know that was my car?" I asked, my steps faltering on the carpet.

"You just told me," he answered as I stopped in the doorway of his office. "*Willkommen zu Kontakt*, Miss Matthews."

The man before me was a German god. Standing behind his desk, he knew exactly who he was and what he wanted out of life. He snapped the cuffs on his white dress shirt, his black blazer abandoned on his chair. He wore a ring on the middle finger of his left hand, but that wasn't what drew my attention. My attention was focused solely on his eyes. Blue. Sky blue. Piercing blue. I sucked in air when they flicked over me from top to bottom and back to top. The forced break in eye contact allowed me to drink in the rest of him.

Perfectly straight nose - check. Strong chin with a tiny cleft to make you swoon - check. Barely-there blond petite goatee - check. Mmm, he was yummy. His blond hair was styled in the mussed, au naturale look, but I suspected he spent a lot of time styling it that way. He was over six feet of lean muscle and under two hundred pounds. I stared at the way his abs and pecs filled out his dress shirt in the most delicious way. He definitely spent his fair share of time at the gym.

"*Schön sie kennenzulermen*, Mr. Jäger." It was indeed extremely nice to meet him. He was sexy with a side of *yes, please*. Even if I didn't get the job, he made the drive over here worth it.

"I am glad you could make it on such short notice." He held up his finger and turned to the bookcase behind him. He fiddled rather clumsily with a camera while he spoke. "I hope you do not mind, but I will be recording our interview."

"Why do you deny your accent?" My head was cocked to the side when he spun on me. "It must be torture."

His highly sculpted brow went up in surprise. "A gutsy little *blauer vogel*."

I noted his accent was strong and free with those words and I grinned in response. "I assure you, I'm no blue bird. The gutsy bit is accurate. Now then, if you'd like to turn the camera off, we can proceed."

He shook his finger at me and then motioned me into the office. "The camera is to protect both of us. If you would like to record it on your own device, that would be acceptable."

I glanced back at the door to judge the distance to safety. "What exactly do I need protecting from?"

He motioned his hand around the office. "It is the nature of the business we'll be discussing. It is better to have clear evidence that our discussion was purely business."

"What else would it be?" He offered me a smile that was meant to be welcoming and reassuring but came off like the Big Bad Wolf's. "I'm afraid I'm at a disadvantage here, Mr. Jäger," I paused when he held up his hand.

"Lars, please."

"Lars. I don't know what kind of business you conduct. I was simply told to be here at three for an interview."

He motioned for me to sit opposite his desk and then lowered his beautifully sculpted German backside into his leather executive chair. I glanced at the camera, back at the door, and then back at him. He was waiting patiently, his hands folded over his desk, and a brow crooked up lazily. It was sexy to the nth degree, and he knew it. I lowered myself to the chair and dug out my resume slowly to give my brain time to restart after that little display of hotness. Still unsure of the situation, I slid my pepper spray into the front pouch of my purse at the same time.

"My resume," I explained, holding it out to him.

"Your resume is not needed. I know that you are graduating summa cum laude on Friday with a marketing degree as well as an honors in German degree."

I tipped my head to the side. "And you know this how?"

He leaned forward onto his desk and eyed me. "Who told you about the interview, Miss Matthews?"

"Serenity, please," I responded with slight irritation in my tone, but not at him. I was irritated with the person who had sent me on this wild goose chase. "My professor told me about the interview. He indicated he didn't know anything about your company, though."

He smiled, his perfectly straight white teeth glinting back at me for a moment. I suspected it was a smile many beautiful women had seen right before he deflowered them. "I spoke with Professor Watkins at length about the position. I am honestly quite surprised you are here. He did not think you would be interested. He indicated that we had not spoken?"

I shook my head to clear it. I wasn't used to his formal way of speaking English. It was his second language, so it wasn't unusual that he didn't use contractions, but it did take some getting used to. I replayed the conversation with Maynard through my head again. I frowned, and immediately his eyes danced with victory. "Actually, he said he didn't need to check you out since you were using a big-name headhunting site."

He tossed his head back and laughed in a manner that told me he was truly tickled. His long neck stretched toward me, and his Adam's apple bobbed just enough to remind me of his virility. He was all man, and I was struggling to follow our conversation in the face of it. "He may have had it backward. I was headhunting you, once I knew you existed, that is. I noticed you earlier this month at the Campus Clubs event for the incoming freshman. You are exactly the woman I need for this position."

I cleared my throat and folded my hands in my lap. I prayed my nervousness wasn't as apparent as it felt. "Maybe you shouldn't tell your applicant that. It might give them the wrong idea about negotiations for the position. Maynard indicated you were looking for someone with little to no experience. I'd like to know why that is. It would make more sense to employ someone with extensive knowledge of marketing when you're trying to get a company off the ground."

The left side of his lips tipped up in a motion that made me want to drop my panties instantly and let him have his way with me. I bet he was an animal in bed. His eyes told me he knew it, too. "Any other CEO might agree with you, but my business is different than most. The person I hire as a marketing director must be open, flexible, and not tied down to what may have worked for them in the past. My vision for Kontakt will require a fresh new eye and a strong desire to learn new techniques."

"And your business is different how?" I glanced around the office space, but clues were not forthcoming.

"Kontakt involves sensual issues."

"Sensual issues?"

"Mm, that is what I said, Serenity. Now you understand the need for the video camera."

I ran my tongue across my teeth while my eyes darted to the camera and back to him. "You want me to market sensual issues?"

He chuckled, and this time, it was light and airy. "No, I want you to market sensual products. Personal care items. Sensual aids."

"Sensual aids?"

He tipped his head and raised a brow in agreement. "Kontakt designs, manufactures, and sells sensual products for the modern man and woman."

I tapped my chin and forced the embarrassment from my cheeks before they could stain pink. "Let's decipher that statement. Kontakt designs, manufactures, and sells sex toys for any man or woman with enough money to buy one off the internet."

His grin lit up his face, and I sucked in a breath at the idea that he was interviewing me for a position to market vibrators. "We prefer not to use that specific term, but," he paused and waved his hand, "essentially, you are correct."

"Is there something wrong with the term *sex toy*?"

He leaned forward again on his desk, and I instinctively leaned back. "It is outdated, my little *blauer vogel.* Kontakt uses German engineering to design and manufacture products women all over the world are using to awaken their sexual beings. When a woman has a Kontakt aid, she does not need a man to satisfy her. She can do it alone. While that is true, so it is true that many of our products are designed to be used by couples when together."

I refused to drop eye contact with him. What was with him calling me a blue bird all the time? It was wholly inappropriate during a job interview. "Sounds like you're designing, manufacturing, and selling your way out of existence, Lars."

A smile tipped his lips, and it was the evil twin of the one he wore earlier. "If that camera was not on, I would educate you on how untrue that is. Since it is recording, let us discuss the job requirements."

I dug out my notepad and crossed my legs, waiting patiently.

"The building, as you can see, is empty. I am in the process of sorting through the Miami applicants for the positions of marketing director, an assistant to the CEO, a receptionist for the building, and several other clerical positions. The rest of my team will be arriving from Germany in short order."

"Team?" I asked, glancing up from the notebook.

His smile was patient, but there was an underlying impatience I suspected he tamped down often. "Engineers, designers, and excellent visionaries in the field."

Did he own this whole building?

"Kontakt owns the entire building." This time his smile was self-assured. "Each floor will house a different part of the process. All of our aids are handmade and tested thoroughly before they leave our hands. For that reason, I need my engineers to be here to train the new team. This floor holds my private office along with the offices of my inner circle. The tenth floor is my penthouse."

I whistled. "I was wrong. You have made it to the top."

"Never doubt me. It would be wise to remember that, Serenity."

The way he said my name sent a shiver down my spine every time. It made me wonder what it would sound like moaned into my ear.

"Your duties would require you to work at any and all hours of the day or night. Germany is ahead of our time zone, so we must be available to them when they need us, whether it is lunchtime or bedtime. Understood?"

"Understood," I answered, tapping my pen on the notepad. "However, I live forty minutes from here …"

He held up a thin, perfectly manicured finger. "That would have to change." In the next breath, he held out a binder with the company logo on it. The scripted K was gold with filigree surrounding it and gave no indication of what the company actually sold. I don't know what I was expecting. Dildos forming the letter T? A cock ring for the O? I bit back a snort at my own joke and opened the binder. The list of duties told me they would be copious and slightly overwhelming for a new graduate. When I turned the page to the benefits section, I gasped.

"You're offering me an apartment in the building?" I glanced up in surprise, and his blue eyes were laser-focused on my cleavage. I resisted the urge to tug my top up and waited for him to answer.

His fingers steepled, and he tapped them on his lips. "I am not offering. I am insisting."

I finished reading the folder and sat in shock for several beats. An apartment, company car, full benefits, and my student loans paid off if I stay for the term of the one-year contract. That didn't account for the salary that had more zeros behind it than I'd ever seen in my lifetime.

"Wow." The word was meant to be strong, but it was high pitched and squeaky. "Sensual products must be a hot commodity. This is …"

He flicked a hand at the binder dismissively. "The package is based on your expertise in both my language and culture, as well as your marketing degree. There is little I do not already know about you, Serenity. My extensive research tells me you know the offer is fair and better than you would get working for any other company."

"On the contrary, Lars, there is much you don't know about me."

Like how your eyes get me all hot and bothered and how my fingers want to mess up your hair for real.

"I hope I have many opportunities to learn those things while you are working at Kontakt." He didn't intend for it to sound erotic, but the timbre of his voice made it so.

I swallowed and tapped the folder. "You were serious about the headhunting." He tipped his head in answer. "Can I have some time to think about this?"

"Of course, take all the time you need."

I stowed my items back in my purse and stood, reaching my hand across the desk to shake his one last time. "Thank you, Lars. I'll be in touch."

He stood from behind his desk and shook my hand, leaving little tingles of sex flowing through my veins. When he dropped my hand, I strode to the door, knowing his eyes were now trained on my perfectly rounded backside.

He called my name, and when I turned, he wore the smile of a man who never questioned if he would get what he wanted. He would. "I will see you tomorrow at nine a.m."

I didn't respond, but I hated that he knew me so well this early in the game.

I plowed through the front door and dropped my bag on the floor. "Professor!" I yelled while I stormed through the kitchen. I didn't notice Babette until she cleared her throat.

"You better take a moment and simmer down," she tisked without turning from the stove. "You know Maynard won't deal with that redheaded temper of yours."

I huffed, but my feet stopped their mad stomp through the house. "The hair is fake, but the temper is one hundred percent real."

Her shoulders shook with laughter while she stirred her big pot of bubbling goodness. "The hair is as real as the temper, but a valiant effort, *fiy*."

My temper flickered and died with her nickname for me. *Fiy* meant daughter in Louisiana Creole, which was Babette's proud heritage. I kissed her cheek and then peeked in the pot. My mouth watered at the savory scents wafting from it. "Mmm, chicken creole."

"What else would we have to celebrate your final test at college?"

Her accent was still strong after all these years of living away from Louisiana, and it made me think of Lars. Would his accent always be as strong as it was today after living in the States for years? That thought made me think of his sexy eyes, well-defined chest, and finely filled out trousers. I rubbed my thighs together and moaned slightly. I had to stop!

I focused on the woman who, over the last three years, had been my mother and confidant. I grinned with excitement. "Can you believe it? I'm done! D O N E!" I spelled while dancing around her.

She giggled and threw her arms around me, offering a motherly hug of congratulations. "We knew you could do it. Your determination was why we let you live here and put up with that temper of yours all these years." She winked lovingly, and I knew she was kidding, but she was actually dead on. I had a temper, and I didn't always think before I let it rip. "Now, little *fiy*, why are you mad at my Maynard."

Her words made me think of how Lars called me his little blue bird. I stepped out of her embrace and grabbed a can of Dr. Pepper. I took a healthy gulp before I answered her question. "He sent me off on an interview today and wasn't exactly honest about the situation."

"That doesn't sound like my Maynard," she insisted, adding more spice to her pot of chicken, tomatoes, and garlic.

"Try not to think of it as dishonest but rather as not forthcoming," Professor Maynard Watkins pontificated as he strode through the door

The man before me was well under six feet tall and well over three hundred pounds. It was three years ago when he found me sleeping in a tent at the back of the campus. He immediately dragged me home to Babette like a mangy stray dog.

I planted a hand on my hip and glared at him from where I sat. "That's basically the same thing!"

He kissed his wife on the cheek, and she shooed him to the table while she scooped her spicy chicken into bowls. "As I was saying," he said after he sat down, "the two are not the same thing. They're actually quite different."

I lowered a brow and glared at him. "They both mean you didn't tell me what I was walking into."

"The way I see it, I did. I gave you his name, the company's name, and when to be there. I was honest about that part. I was less than forthcoming with the rest on purpose."

"You purposely wanted me to be embarrassed in Lars Jäger's office?" My tone was snippy, and he snickered. Snickered!

"I thought it would be better for him to explain the company to you. I didn't want you to be put off and not go to the interview."

"Put off?" Babette asked from the stove. "Put off by what?"

"Kontakt sells sensual aids, Babette. It would be my job to market them here in the States."

Her spoon clanked against the side of the metal pot. "Sensual aids? What on earth is a sensual aid?"

I threw my arms up in the air. "Sex toys, Babette! Sex toys!"

"Oh dear," she said, but I could see she was forcing back the laughter wanting to spill out.

"You both think I'm a prude." I huffed and took another sip of my Dr. Pepper.

"No," Maynard insisted, "but I know for sure that you're stubborn. If I thought you were a prude, I never would have sent you to the interview."

"You think you know me so well," I hissed, and he sat back against the tall, cane backed chair of the less formal dining set Babette kept in the kitchen.

"Let me ask you a question. If Kontakt sold pencils, would we be having this discussion?"

"That's a ridiculous question. You know we wouldn't be. Everyone needs pencils. They market themselves."

"I taught you one rule of marketing," he said, and I rolled my eyes.

"I know, pencils and toilet paper are the only two things that can market themselves," I repeated.

He smiled with happiness that his lessons had stuck. "Then my question is, are you afraid of a little hard work?"

I lowered my brow, and Babette snickered from where she was scooping out the rice into dishes. "Afraid of hard work? Hardly."

"What is it then that's keeping you from taking this once in a lifetime opportunity?" he asked. "Maybe you are a prude?"

I huffed and crossed my arms over my chest. "I'm not a prude."

He grinned and held up his finger. "Are you afraid to tell people that you market sensual aids?"

"I sat in your lectures for three years. Do you honestly think I forgot the one you gave the most?" I asked, sitting up and preparing my fake professor's voice. "If you can't market yourself, then you better find a new career."

He smiled and winked at me. "Someone has to market sensual aids, Serenity. Obviously, people are buying them. Lars didn't buy an entire office building on credit."

I tapped the table and chewed over what he said. "I guess that's true."

He pointed at me while wearing a smile. "You pass on this job, and you'll never get another offer like it. Ever."

Babette lowered bowls of spicy chicken down in front of us. "Did you pass on the job before you left the interview, *fiy*?"

I grabbed my fork before I answered. "No, I asked him for time to think about it."

"How much time did Lars give you?" Maynard asked.

I smiled hesitantly and lowered my fork. "He said I could take all the time I needed. Then he said he'd see me tomorrow morning at nine."

They both chuckled, and Babette squeezed my hand the way a mother does. "Sounds settled to me then, no?"

"I want the job, but …"

"But?"

"But why me? He seriously headhunted me!" I exclaimed in a hushed voice.

Maynard leaned forward and held my eye. "I don't find that hard to believe. Neither should you. You're fantastic at marketing, brilliant at the German language, and even better at reading people. You were made for this position."

"You think so?" They both nodded in unison. I smiled shyly before I blew out a breath. "Well, then I guess you're looking at the new marketing director for Kontakt."

Babette tapped her fork on the table twice in a proclamation. "It is official! Let's eat good food and celebrate you!"

I grabbed my fork and when the first bite of chicken hit my tongue, I moaned. My pleasure was tempered by the knowledge that accepting Lars Jäger's offer meant I had to leave these two fabulous people behind.

Two

Lars

The view from the tenth floor varied depending on where you were standing. To the west was the concrete jungle, and to the east, which happened to be where my bedroom sat, was tranquility. The bedroom overlooked lush greenery and a trickling stream flowing through it. I ate breakfast on the balcony before work every day, and in the evening, it was a place for dinner parties and quiet dates. It was only a matter of time before I would spend much of my free time entertaining in the penthouse and I looked forward to it. The dating part, however, would not come to fruition. I allowed occasional rolls in the hay with beautiful women interested in nothing more than sex, but my life had no place for anything else.

I focused my attention to the west and trained my eyes on the empty parking spot next to my car. Would my little blue bird step up and accept the position, or would she be too afraid of what a company like Kontakt would do to both her reputation and her sex life? The look she wore during the interview I had seen many times as CEO of Kontakt. As soon as the product is revealed, the stain of either shame or embarrassment creeps slowly from their necks to their cheeks.

I noticed it for the first time when I was fourteen. I wanted to know why, so I asked my *mutter*. We had an open relationship, and she did not hesitate to give me an honest answer. She said women are taught their bodies are not for their pleasure, but for a man's pleasure. If a woman were to openly admit to pleasuring themselves, they would be ridiculed. I asked why a man was not equally ridiculed for the same, and her answer surprised me. She said it was expected that a man would pleasure himself, so it was readily accepted. As a young man, I could not understand such a double standard. Those two questions resulted in the most honest conversation I had ever had with anyone in my life, even if that person was the woman who gave birth to me. She answered my questions without redness staining her cheeks or shame filling her eyes. Now, I understood it was to prepare me to run the family business, and to offer me a positive introduction to sex and sexuality. I grew up steeping in body and sexual positivity, but it was immediately evident to me that most other humans, women especially, were not. For every overtly sexual woman I met, I was aware there were hundreds of others who were hiding their true sexual desires. Now, I see it as my mission to teach women it is not embarrassing or shameful to pleasure themselves. For if we do not love ourselves, who will?

I was sure of one thing when Serenity left my office yesterday, she would be the one to move this company forward in the United States. I was also sure I would have to teach her how to love herself before that would happen. She was delightfully uptight during the interview and my fingers ached to pull the pin from her bun holder. I fantasized about watching that fiery red hair fall to her shoulders. She was beautiful. If I dated, she would be on the top of my card.

Her German heritage was evident in her blue eyes and her Irish heritage in her red hair. Her cheeks were chiseled, and her lips were pink, puckered, and aching to be kissed. The way her tongue darted out to lick them, leaving a sheen of wetness across them each time, made my cock pulse against my zipper with wanton desire. I was never more grateful to be sitting down than I was yesterday when she lowered herself to the chair and crossed one tanned leg over the other. They were shapely and thin, and her high heels displayed a set of red-painted toes that left me more than a little hot under the collar. My mind wandered to her wearing nothing but those high heels in my bed. I rubbed the hardness inside my suit pants, and my eyes darted to my dresser drawer where our latest sensual aid prototype was hidden. If only I had the time, I would work out my frustrations with it before I went to the office.

    My attention back on the clock, my lips tugged down into a frustrated frown. It was well after nine-thirty and Serenity had not arrived. Either she was purposely late to prove she would not be bossed around, or she would not be accepting the position. It was a shame she did not have the common courtesy to send an email.

    My desire for the woman died instantly at the thought. Finally able to walk again, I snapped my cuffs and stepped into my private elevator. There was no point in standing around waiting for her. I would have to regroup and find someone else who could do the job. I was all too aware that it was likely going to require more work than it did to find Miss Matthews. I had lucked into her rather quickly. The same would not be true a second time.

Indeed, my office was dead quiet when I stepped off the elevator, so I lowered myself to my desk chair and sighed. I had no other prospects in the U.S., and bringing someone over from Germany would defeat the purpose. I needed someone who understood the habits of the American woman in order to be successful here. I was aware my company was not typical, but with the package I put together, I was sure it would be a, how do they say it here, no brainer? Maybe I underestimated Serenity Matthews after all. I might have let her past skew my assessment of how far she would go to make a better life for herself. It was apparent I would have to do more to woo her.

I hit the power button for my computer and resolved to put together a package she could not refuse. Hating myself for it, I checked my email on my phone while I waited for the computer to load. No email and she was ... I checked the clock ... forty-five minutes late. I had little time to convince her to work for me before the owner of the company flew over here and reamed me out for disappointing her. Nepotism was not in my *mutter's* vocabulary, and I was not about to test her leniency.

I stood and stuck my hand in my hair, determined to think of something I could offer Serenity that would convince her working for Kontakt was what she wanted. I offered her a car, an apartment, and the opportunity to be debt-free. What was left? I dropped my hand to my leg. I could remove the clause that she remains here for one year. It was a risk, but paying off her student loans as a bonus was a small price to pay.

The sun glinted off something below my window and nearly blinded me. It only took one glance at the parking lot, and my feet were moving. I was out the door and running down the stairs at a speed in which I had forgotten I could run. I pushed my way through the glass doors and never slowed as I ran toward her. She was struggling to get out of the car, one leg in and one leg out, a broken heel dangling on the one hanging out.

"Serenity!" I called as I approached so as not to scare her already shell-shocked face. "Are you okay?"

She was out of the car and limping toward me now, her messenger bag hanging at her side. Her dress was torn and dirty in multiple different places, and she walked with a limping halt on the broken heel. By the time I reached her, she was ready to collapse, and I grasped her elbows to help her into the building. Once she was sitting on the bench, I knelt in front of her. One look into her eyes told me she was not okay.

I held my hand on her shoulder and grabbed my phone. "Sit still. I am calling an ambulance."

She swung her head back and forth. "No, I already declined one. Please. I can't afford it," she said desperately, struggling to stand again.

My phone still in my hand, I held her in place. "What happened?"

She wasn't concentrating on my questions. Instead, she muttered about her shoes, her dress, and what her hair must look like. "I can't believe I was late for my first day of work."

My heart did a double-tap in my chest. She wants the job. I had to stop myself from doing, what do you call it, a fist yank? She wants the job! One look at her told me she was not in any shape to work at the moment, though. I stood and scooped her up out of the chair into my arms. She shrieked and grabbed at my neck when I strode to the elevator. I punched the button and waited impatiently for the doors to open.

She swatted at my chest with her hand. "Lars, put me down. I can walk!" she exclaimed multiple times, in both English and German, in case I needed to understand it bilingually.

"You are dazed, confused, dirty, disheveled, and scraped. I am taking you to my apartment until I decide if you need a hospital."

She moaned, and her head flopped onto my shoulder at the mention of a hospital. "I'm fine. If you'd kindly unhand me, I'll go home and change. When I get back, we can get to work."

I stood in silence, not unhanding her, and impatiently counting off the floors on the ride up. She huffed every few seconds that I refused to put her down until the door opened to the tenth floor. I used my back to push open an apartment door across from mine and lowered her to the couch. I motioned for her to stay put and jogged to the small bathroom for a cool, wet washcloth. By the time I returned, she had removed the broken shoes and was brushing at her dress in disbelief. She did not question where I got the towel from, simply ran it around her face and neck, then wiped her hands with it. After a moment, she scooted to the end of the couch. "Okay, I'm ready to go. Where do we start?"

I held my hands out to her rather than touch her again. Every time I did, something in me flared bright and hot. She made parts of me tick that had not ticked in the last fifteen years. It was an uncomfortable and disconcerting feeling to experience again. I did not enjoy being uncomfortable. That was the reason I had avoided intimate relationships to begin with.

"We start by making sure you are not injured and do not need a doctor."

She shook her head so wildly she fell back against the couch. "I'm fine."

I held up her left arm. It was covered in road rash and blood, and the way she held it told me it was painful.

She sighed heavily. "Maybe not fine fine, but I don't need a doctor. I'll go home, clean up, and come back. Give me thirty minutes. No, maybe I'll need an hour."

"How do you plan to get home, my little *blauer vogel*? Your car is shuddering its last breath as we speak."

Her shoulders slumped in resignation, and for the first time, I noticed she was sitting funny. She held her left side off the couch, and I moved behind her to see that half of her dress was missing. The entire left side of her body was bleeding from road rash.

"*Verdammt!*" I exclaimed angrily. "Tell me what happened, right now," I demanded when I faced her again.

The eyes that should have widened at my anger stared straight ahead. "I got a flat tire and was on the side of the road trying to decide if I needed to call someone. A car lost control and sideswiped me before I could blink. When it hit, I was knocked backward and skidded across the gravel on the road."

"You did not let them take you to the hospital after you were hit by a car?" I asked, my voice an octave lower than usual from the anger inside me.

"I'm fine," she insisted. I lowered a brow at her. "I'm fine, considering I could be dead. Is that better?"

"Not especially." Her eyes clouded, and pain was evident on her face. She was in shock, and I forced myself to stop being an asshole for a few minutes. "Did the car hit you, Serenity?"

She shook her head again, less wildly this time. "Not that car, no. I was standing on the passenger side of my car inspecting the tire. The other car pushed my car into me and sent me flying. I'll be okay after a shower and some clean clothes. I'm sorry I'm late, Lars. I even left early to make sure I arrived on time."

I squatted next to her and held her gaze. "You cannot control these things, Serenity. What matters is that you are still alive. I am going to call a doctor to come here and check you over. Your arm could be broken."

She struggled to stand, but I rested my hands on her thighs, forcing my mind away from her soft skin and the warmth soaking into my fingers. "I can't see a doctor," she said again, "I don't have any insurance. The driver that hit me didn't have any, either."

I cursed under my breath. How typical is that? A bad driver who does not carry insurance. "Serenity, are you accepting the position at Kontakt?" I asked, forcing her to focus on my voice.

She nodded her head up and down in a daze. "Yes, that's why I'm here. You said to be here at nine. I'm sorry for being so late."

I squeezed her legs gently until she quieted. "Do you accept the terms of the contract, as we discussed yesterday?" She nodded again, the fight slowly draining away as pain and fatigue overtook it. "Then you are officially an employee of Kontakt, which means you have insurance and can see a doctor. I know you will not allow an ambulance, but will you accept me driving you to the hospital?"

She moaned and shook her head, tears gathering in her eyes. "No, I don't want to go to the hospital, Lars. I'm fine. We need to get to work."

"We have time to make sure you are not in pain before we work. How about a compromise?" I asked while she shifted uncomfortably again. "I will call a doctor to come here and clean your wounds. Then you can shower and change here. Is that acceptable?"

"Where are we?" she asked, gazing around the room. "Wait, I don't have any clothes with me. I could call Babette and ask her to bring me some. Yeah, that might work."

I held up my finger and picked up my phone. She did not disagree with the doctor coming here, so I wanted to get someone on their way over. I knew just the person, too. I placed a call while she closed her eyes and grimaced when her shoulder touched the couch. I hung up the phone and grasped her shoulders carefully, leading her toward the small bedroom.

"This is your apartment. Do you remember when we talked about that?" I asked, and she nodded automatically. I lowered her to the bed, and she laid over on her right side. I doubted her story about how hard the car had hit her. She was too out of it to not have taken a knock to the head.

"It's a charming little place. I don't need a doctor, seriously," she murmured.

I patted her shoulder to calm her. I truly believed she needed more than just a doctor. She needed a hospital, but I could tell I would not convince her of that. Why did this little skiff of a woman bring out the protector in me instantly? Only one other person had ever brought those emotions to the surface so quickly and considering he was dead, that was not a good thing.

"The doctor is on her way. We are going to make sure you are healthy and not in pain before we do any work. Please, relax until she arrives." I stood and slid open a door on the wall then snapped on a light. "I have made sure you have a full wardrobe here, as I suspected you did not have enough for a job such as this one."

Slowly, she sat up and tossed her feet onto the floor, standing with an unsteady tilt. I grasped her arm carefully and helped her walk to the closet. "How did you know my size?" She shuffled through the dresses, pantsuits, and skirts.

"It was not difficult, Serenity. I used a personal consultant who assured me you would find these items acceptable. At least until you can shop for what you would like."

She turned and eyed me. "Are you serious? These are beautiful designer brands. I can only dream about owning clothing this beautiful. I can't accept them. There must be thousands of dollars in clothing here. Look at the shoes," she exclaimed. She turned too quickly to point at the shoes lining the wall and ended up in my arms when she tipped over.

Her eyes rolled back in her head, and I half carried her to the bed to lay her down. "Nonsense, Serenity. You certainly can accept it, but right now, you need to rest." She grimaced when the bed touched a sore spot, and I rested my hand on her hip. "I am going to get you some ice and bring the doctor up. Just rest now."

I rubbed her hip until her eyes closed and she dropped off to sleep. I propped a pillow carefully behind her back, so she did not roll onto the road rash. When I left the room, her beautiful face was surrounded by her red hair flowing across the pillow. It was too much for my groin to handle when it knew it could never have her.

<u>Three</u>

Serenity

I think that car punted me into the Twilight Zone. The doctor had come and treated my cuts and scrapes, I had taken a shower in what was my new bathroom filled with all my favorite products, and dressed in clothing I could only dream about buying before today. I hurt everywhere, but I refused to spend the rest of the day doing anything but what I came here to do. Work.

    I stepped off the elevator and grit my teeth together to avoid limping toward his office. I hadn't broken anything, but the doctor was sure I had sprained my wrist and ankle. I had a brace on both, so I was praying a good part of today was going to be spent sitting down. My head pounded, and I squinted one eye half-closed to block out some of the light.

"I feel like I left home three hours ago as Serenity Matthews and woke up as Goldilocks," I said, stopping in the doorway to his office.

He was at the door in one fluid motion of his hard, chiseled body. The body I had been pressed up against just a few hours earlier. I had wanted to stay in his arms as much as I had wanted to get out of them. I wasn't sure what to do with that other than to pretend it didn't happen.

"How are you feeling?" he asked, taking my upper arm carefully and helping me to the large conference table. He pulled a chair out for me and helped me sit, then grabbed his laptop and joined me at the table.

"I'm hurting, but the doctor says I'll live. Thank you for all of that," I said, pointing upward. "I think I was in shock and probably wasn't making good decisions."

He lowered a brow at me. "Probably?"

I laughed then, and the release was needed for both of us. "You're right. I was knocked a little bit silly. The doctor said I don't have a concussion, so that's good news, right?"

He nodded once. "She did say you have a sprained wrist and ankle, though. You could take it easy today and ice them down. I would not be upset."

I brushed my hand at him. "As long as it isn't strenuous work, I'll be fine. I will need to deal with the old car later. Maybe I should call Maynard?"

"Done and done," he said, opening the laptop.

"You called Maynard, or you dealt with the car?" I asked, suddenly on edge.

"Both. I wanted the professor to know you were okay in case you had called him in the state you were in. He said he would call you when class was done."

I glanced at the clock and figured that would be in about an hour. "And the car?"

"He told me to put her out of her misery, so I had a tow truck pick the car up an hour ago. All your belongings are over there." He pointed to a box in the corner.

I sighed. "That's all that's left of the old girl, huh? She didn't deserve to go out that way."

"I assume you have had the car for some time?" he asked, leaning back and resting an ankle over his knee. I noted immediately he wore socks with his dress shoes. Thank God. Nothing made me nuttier than men wearing dress shoes without socks. I know it's the whole Miami Vice look, but that look died years ago.

"Actually, only about three years. It was Maynard's daughter's car originally. She drove it through high school and college until she bought a new one. They handed it down to me so I could get to class and work. It wasn't worth anything by then, and Maynard insisted I drive it."

"That was kind of them."

"If it wasn't for their kindness, I probably wouldn't have made it through college. They didn't have to take me in. I most likely owe them my life."

"I doubt they feel that way, Serenity."

I shrugged. "Maybe not, but all the same, I know how I got to where I am today."

"Hard work and determination from what I can see. The Watkins did not have to house you, but they also did not do the work required to be where you are today."

I tipped my head. "I haven't told them I'm moving out. After seeing the apartment today, I suppose it's time I do that."

"Maynard is aware of what the benefits are for this position. It was posted on the website he had access to. He will not be surprised, but yes, it would be wise to tell him you will be staying here now."

I sighed and did the palms up. "I guess so since I no longer have a car."

He held up his finger and pulled the laptop over in front of us. "That is the first item on the agenda for today.

"We're going car shopping? You don't have fleet vehicles?"

He started tapping buttons while he answered. "No, you will choose your own car. Luckily, we can buy the car online, and they will deliver it. I do not want you going out today."

For the next hour, we sat at the table and narrowed down cars until we settled on an Audi A7 with all the bells and whistles. He literally paid for it online and scheduled the delivery for this evening. I had objected to the price every time he brought up a car, but in the end, he told me if I didn't choose, he would. After much discussion about what cars were German-made, we settled on the Audi, though I was open about my discomfort with the expense.

He closed the laptop and settled it back on his desk before he turned to me. It wasn't the first time I noticed how nicely he filled out both the back and the front of his pants. The pants hugged him in all the right places, and it was easy to tell he didn't buy his clothes off the rack. Those pants were tailored for him. Even though I shouldn't stare, I decided someone had to appreciate them.

"Are you feeling up to interviews this afternoon? I have several lined up for my personal assistant position as well as the downstairs receptionist and building manager. If you are not well, you may retire to your apartment."

I held up my finger. "About the apartment."

"Do you not find it acceptable?" His tone was cordial with a hint of displeasure.

I stood and limped toward him. He leaned against his desk casually, and his German God look had never been stronger. "It's a beautiful apartment, Lars. I simply wanted to thank you for the furnished space. I wasn't sure how I was going to furnish a place, but then you probably knew that, right?"

"It was logical considering you did not live alone previously, which is why I put it in the contract. The contract that you have not signed yet." This time his tone was unsure even though he had just purchased me a seventy-thousand-dollar car.

"You're right, I planned to do that when I arrived, but ..." I waved my hand at the windows. "Should I sign it now?"

The look that crossed his handsome face was one of relief, and I made a note of it. He may not have been lying when he said he had no one else for this position.

He held up the contract and lowered it to the table before handing me a pen. I scrawled my name on the bottom of both pages and patted it twice. "I guess that makes me an official employee of Kontakt."

He accepted the pen when I held it out, and his fingers caressed mine when he slid it from them. His skin was soft, warm, and left little pinpricks of sex across my skin. I wondered what it would feel like to have those hands wrapped around my hips while he called out my name in ecstasy.

Oh man, what did I just do? Now I had to work with the sexiest man alive while strategizing how to sell sex toys. I also had to pretend to know everything about sex when the exact opposite was true. While he continued to gaze at me with those sexy and searching blue eyes, I was sure of one thing. If you checked the dictionary for the term *hot mess*, you'd see my picture.

The last three months had been a bit insane. Truthfully, they'd been completely mad, but fantastically so. My graduation was an event to remember, made possible by Babette and Maynard. They had brought their extended family in to fill the bleachers for the event. They all held signs with my head on them while they clanked cowbells and generally carried on with love and encouragement. Walking across the stage and accepting my diploma from Maynard was the best possible way to end that part of my life. The degree was a new beginning, and I was ready to grasp it.

When I stopped for the obligatory picture at the end of the stage, my eyes had drifted to the stands, pulled by an unseen force. My gaze met his where he sat, his Jil Sander suit hugging him like a glove. He sensed the moment I saw him and let that confident smile tip his lips upward. His head nodded once and I smiled without thought. The resulting picture now sits on my mantle. Only he and I understood how that picture had come to be the best one ever taken of me.

The afternoon of my accident, we'd managed to hire Lexie, as an assistant for Lars and a building manager, Seth, who would also be the receptionist. I preferred to call Seth *The Lean Mean We'd Be Screwed Without You Machine*. He made sure Lars and I could keep working on our end of the business by taking care of the rest of the team as they arrived from Germany. He was the reason they were already set up on their respective floors and in full swing this quickly in the process. Seth had also organized the catering company to come in and get the café open on the first floor. While all of that was going on, he prepped and stocked the gym for anyone who wanted to use it.

Since Lars had four apartments on the top floor of the building, all the major players had one. I lived next door to Lexie, his assistant, and she lived next door to Seth. We were across the hall from Lars, who, for all purposes, was either alone behind his office door or alone behind his apartment door. No women, or men for that matter, came in or out, and the only people he ever ate dinner with were Lexie or me.

Lexie was a godsend to both of us when it came to running the office of the CEO, which spilled over into marketing, at least right now. Lars and I worked so closely together she was always able to predict what we needed before we needed it. I could say she had become the first close friend I'd ever had in my life. We spent many nights laughing together while drinking wine in one or the other's apartment. She talked about men and her dates. I mostly bit my tongue to keep from saying something inappropriate about our boss. It was easy to admit to myself in the dark of night, lying in my empty bed alone, that I had a massive crush on the man who controlled my life. Unfortunately, or fortunately, depending on how you look at it, I would never be able to fulfill those fantasies. There was no way I was screwing up this dream job to scratch an itch. I'd sooner use a sensual aid before I did that.

I shuddered and then snickered. Thus far, I had avoided that awkward situation, and I was glad for it. The last thing I wanted to do was admit I didn't even know how to turn one on. My phone rang and I grabbed it, answering while I stacked the folders I would need when I arrived at Lars' office. "This is Serenity."

"Serenity," my boss's deep voice said my name in a way that always sent shivers of sex down my spine, "would you come to my office?"

I cleared my throat before I spoke. The last thing I wanted to do was croak like an idiot. Then he would know exactly how much he affected me. "I was just on my way."

I didn't wait for a response, just dropped the receiver in the cradle, grabbed my papers, and sashayed down the hallway with a sassy spring in my step. I was about to make his day!

Four

I rapped once on the door, and his deep *come in* made me shudder again. I waited for it to pass before I closed the door behind me and set the folders on the table by his desk.

"My little *blauer vogel,* you must be quite excited to have hung up on your boss." When he stood, I noticed his sleeves were rolled to his elbows, giving me a clear shot of his muscular forearms sprinkled with fine blond hair. He was hot as hell, and his silver Cartier strapped to his wrist, added to the mystique. The watch was his grandfather's, that much I knew. His mother had given it to him on his twenty-first birthday. It hadn't left his wrist in the nine years since. It was when I realized he was six years older than me that I vowed never to let on about the crush I had on him. That was more experience than I could handle. Not that experience is bad, but a thirty-year-old man with extensive sexual knowledge and a twenty-four-year-old virgin weren't going to be compatible. Besides, I'd heard there were plenty of guys out there who liked nothing more than to take a woman's virginity and walk away. I couldn't say Lars was one of them, but I certainly didn't want to find out after a roll in the hay. Don't get me wrong. It would probably be a star-studded, toy-filled, mind-blowing roll in the hay extravaganza, but I wasn't about to find out.

He strode around the desk, kissed my cheek, and motioned for me to sit at the table. I had come to accept that the cheek kissing was just part of his culture, and that would never change. He explained his chosen nickname for me over dinner one night. He said the first time he saw me I was wearing a blue shirt and was as small as a bird. When I pointed out that bluebird in German was *drossel*, he just smiled and continued on with his way of doing it. I kind of liked that he had an endearing nickname for me now.

"Sorry about that," I said sheepishly as I sat and flipped the folder open. "I couldn't wait to tell you that we secured Eternally Sensual Boutique. Not just the main boutique, either! All of their sister boutiques throughout Miami and the surrounding counties are part of the deal!"

He glanced down at the paperwork and then back to me several times. *"Ich glaub mich knutscht ein elch!"*

He was genuinely excited, and it tickled something inside me to know I was responsible for that emotion. "I can't believe it either, to be honest. They were a hard sell and I didn't think we'd pull it off."

He grasped my shoulder and held my gaze. His was a steamy, dreamy stare of pride. There was something else, but I refused to let myself go there. I refused to let myself believe it was desire that also shined in his eyes. "I knew you would pull it off. That is why I hired you, Serenity. I did not think anything could top the news I got earlier, but this has!"

He stood and grabbed me, pulling me into one of his rare, but sweet, bear hugs. "You did good, *blauer vogel.*"

I dropped my arms to my side and froze in place. I didn't want to hug this man. That would only drive the dreams I had of him deeper into my subconscious, where they would torture me every night instead of every other night. His arms fell away then, and he snapped back into Lars, the CEO.

I hugged my arms to my waist, and he turned and walked toward his desk. "What was the other good news?"

His shoulders were straight and stiff when he turned and leaned on his desk, propping his palms on the edge. "How about if I show you instead?" he asked with a brow raised.

"You know I'm always game for new marketing ideas."

He grasped my arm and walked with me out of his office, stopping by the front desk. "Lexie, Miss Matthews and I will be occupied for several moments. Please hold my calls until further notice."

"Of course," she said, distracted by her computer.

He motioned me toward my office, but halfway down, he grabbed my waist to stop me. In front of us was a storage room he always told me was empty. He swiped his badge across the electronic lock and pushed the door open. I walked inside, and when he clicked on the lights, I almost tripped on my own feet.

I gazed around the room in wonderment. "I guess it's not an empty storage room anymore."

He shook his head and hit another switch, illuminating each separate display case around the room. I heard the door latch shut but barely registered it as I took it all in.

"This is our new display room for potential clients," he explained, motioning toward the displays of sensual aids. Each one lay on a velvet pillow with a brushed nickel picture light above it. When he walked past each one, he clicked a remote, and the high-end toy was instantly illuminated. I was sure my cheeks were as red as the velvet covering the pillows, but I refused to break eye contact with him.

I forced myself to turn in a circle and take it all in. "This is one hell of a display, Lars."

"*Danke*. It houses our entire catalog. I hoped to impress you with it."

"Impress me?" I asked stymied when I turned back to face him. He loomed in front of me, and I swallowed hard. Every possible carnal thought came to mind in a split second when I stared into his eyes.

"You are the marketing director, no?" I nodded, my mouth dry, and my body on fire from being this close to him. "Then that makes this your room, not mine. This is where you will work your magic."

"Why didn't you ask for my input?" My voice was far squeakier than I wanted it to be, but I couldn't take the question back now.

His hand came up to grasp my shoulder in a warm embrace. "My little *blauer vogel*, do you think I do not know you are … mmm … should we say, *unerfahren*, no?"

He knows I'm inexperienced. Great. I didn't respond, choosing instead to walk around the room and take in the toys as they sat for all to see in their sensual, yet elegant, glory. "I have to say, you've done an excellent job with the display. It's understated, tasteful, and classy."

"Which is Kontakt in three words, Serenity. We strive for all three of those, and I am happy to know I have achieved that look with the room. The aids displayed on the left wall include our newest line of off-the-shelf products."

"These are going to be the mass-produced aids?" I asked, motioning at the various sizes and shapes of toys that I was utterly clueless about. "They're gorgeous."

"Serenity, we do nothing but gorgeous at Kontakt, including the women I surround myself with." I turned away and walked toward the other wall. "The off-the-shelf products will be manufactured here in the building, but each one will still be tested individually to make sure they meet Kontakt's strict quality control."

"And these?" I asked, motioning at the wall in front of me.

He walked up behind me and plastered himself along the whole of me. I could feel the heat radiating through his white dress shirt, and I wanted to turn and brace my hands against his hard chest. I wanted to lay my lips on his and shiver in his arms when his tongue stroked mine. "These are new special-order pieces. They are for the more particular customer."

I cleared my throat and stared at the anatomically correct silicone vibrators and other various aids. "Gotcha. What about these?" I asked, turning and pointing at the case in the center of the room with three shelves. Each shelf displayed two toys in all their gold and silver glory.

He walked to the display and opened the case, reaching in and cradling a gold vibrator. "These are custom made sensual aids. They are for a subset of buyers who surpass even our most particular customers."

"Porn stars?" I joked, and he lowered a brow at me.

"The term is an adult entertainment performer, Serenity. Regardless, it is more likely we will see the wives of some of the most powerful men selecting one of these aids. It is your job to market to that community."

"The rich and powerful? How much are we talking here, Lars?"

A cagey smile lifted his lips upward when he lowered the surprisingly robust vibrator into my hands. The light glinted off the polished gold, and I could see my reflection in the metal. I was sure I looked like a fish out of water standing there. "The one you hold in your perfect little hand is right around fifteen."

"Fifteen? Hundred?"

"Thousand."

"Fifteen thousand dollars?" I squeaked, the metal vibrating from the shaking of my hand. "I'm sorry, but if you can spend fifteen K on a vibrator," his brow went down, "sensual aid, that's when you know you have too much money."

His laughter was almost evident when he lifted the aid from my hand and set it back in the case. "My darling, too much money is not a thing."

I nodded my head vigorously until he had to grasp my chin to stop it. "When you come from my background, too much money is definitely a thing. Why would I spend fifteen thousand dollars on a vibrator that does the same thing a fifteen dollar one does?"

His chin hit his chest and his eyes closed. He sucked in a breath and let it out slowly before he opened his eyes again. I was pretty sure I tried his patience a lot. "In this business, the most dangerous opinion anyone can have is that all sensual aids are the same. I assure you, they are not. For instance," he said, motioning me toward a shelf on the wall to my right. "This is our newest aid for men. We have many as you know, but this aid," he said, lifting down a canister from the shelf and stroking it, dare I say, longingly, "is unlike any other canister stimulator on the market."

"It looks hot, I'll give you that," I agreed, taking in the jet-black canister done in diamond plating. He spun the device around in his deft hands. Oh yeah, he had definitely used this one before. He showed me a cut out window where purple silicone peeked out from inside.

"This is pure pleasure. This is the aid every man, from your everyday Joe to the world's most powerful, wants in their collection."

"What's so great about it?" He opened his mouth to launch into a canned description, and I put my finger against his lips. "Tell me from a man's perspective, not a sales perspective."

He swallowed, and the canister tremored just slightly in his hands. "I am afraid I cannot do that without it coming off completely inappropriate for the workplace."

I held my arms out wide at the two walls. "There is nothing about what we do here that is appropriate for the workplace, Lars. I can't market this to men without firsthand knowledge of how it applies to their lives. I'm not a man, I can't try it."

He raised a brow but must have thought better about what he was going to say. Instead, he set it on the palm of his hand and held it out to me, nodding for me to take it. I grasped the cold metal in my hand, the ridges making the canister easy to hold, even for my small hand.

"We have not reached a final decision on the name for this yet. We will need your input, so let me introduce you to it." He took out his phone, and I lowered a brow until the aid started buzzing in my hand. "This is one of the first app-controlled male stimulators on the market."

"App controlled?" I asked curiously.

He stalked behind me like a panther and held the phone out for me to see. It was set up like a console for a gamer. "Men like to personalize their experience. The app allows them to set-up custom patterns and speeds for the device. Put your hand inside the opening," he ordered. I swallowed hard because he definitely wasn't asking. Once my fingers were inside it, I noticed it pulsed against them. "Most male stimulators are nothing more than a sleeve with ribbing on the inside. Ours is so much more. Rather than a simple vibrating motor, there are coils inside the device that encompass it. Instead of simple vibration like a traditional sensual aid, it offers a three hundred and sixty-degree pulse of pleasure. Using the app, the user can set the speed and pattern to change multiple different times as they climb toward orgasm."

"Fascinating," I whispered. It was, but I was also growing more uncomfortable the longer I stood there with my hand in the device. "That sounded like a website description to me, though. How do I sell this to a guy on the fence about spending ..."

"Three hundred dollars."

I glanced up at him in surprise. His eyes were hawkish and almost black with desire. I had to clear my throat before I spoke. "That's all? I can sell this all day long at that price point."

"Precisely," he agreed. "To help you understand, let me run you through the cycle. Keep your hand inside. What is truly remarkable about this is that the app can show video or stream images during the experience if the user so chooses."

He tapped the screen on his phone, and the pattern changed against my hand. It turned to a slow pulsing rhythm that matched the song playing through his phone's speaker. "Imagine that sensation flowing across the most erotic part of your body right now. Can you imagine that?" he asked in my ear, his words heavy with each syllable. "The moment the pulsing begins, all the man wants is to get lost, and that is where this comes in." He pushed another button, and I almost dropped the canister. There were images of me scrolling across the screen. I waited out the pictures and through the changes of pattern and rhythm on the device with his hot breath blowing against my ear. "Right about now, I am so hard I cannot think, much less stop what is about to happen," he whispers into my ear. "Do you feel the way the tips of your fingers are electrified and pulse from the inside out?" I nodded my head haltingly, and I swear he moaned softly into my ear. "That was my contribution to the project. It is only near the end of the experience that I will get to feel the sensation. My legs start to shake, and my moans of pleasure can no longer be quieted."

The canister jerked softly twice in my hand, the pulsing slowed again, and the rhythm dialed back to almost nonexistent. "After an intense and satisfying orgasm, the device will stroke me for a few moments longer to wring out every last bit of pleasure from the experience before it reverts to standby mode."

I let my hand trail away from the silicone slowly until it was at my side. "That's an incredible piece of technology. I'm a little jealous that I'm not a guy right now."

He lifted the canister from my hand and smiled his wolf's smile while he set it back on the shelf. I didn't miss that his suit pants were tented to the extreme. In the process of averting my eyes when he turned, he strode to me until we stood face-to-face.

"Do not be embarrassed by my reaction. There is not a man alive who can deny his desire for the finer things in life." His gaze raked me from the top of my head to my toes and back to my eyes. "Now that you have experienced what it can do, it is your job to find a name for it."

"The Diamondback," I said immediately and without hesitation.

His brow went up. "Well, well, I am impressed."

"It's my job, Lars. Any red-blooded American male is going to buy something set up like a gaming console that strokes their man meat if it's called The Diamondback."

He lifted a brow and fought back a smile. "Man meat? Classy." I shrugged in defiance of the conversation. "What about the males in other countries?"

I eyed his still tented trousers. "It doesn't appear that will be a problem. Let me amend my statement. Any red-blooded male is going to buy something set up like a gaming console that strokes their man meat, regardless of what it's called."

Another naughty grin slid across his face. "Not untrue. So, how do you say it here? We have hit a homerun?"

I shook my head while I walked to the door. "No, you knocked it out of the park." His resulting smile and wink told me he knew exactly what the saying was. "I have a meeting in three minutes. However, don't think for a moment I've forgotten that my picture was on your app. A discussion will be had at a later date in regards to that matter."

He strode toward me with intent and purpose. "Do not think for a moment I have forgotten that you think a fifteen-thousand-dollar sensual aid is the same as one that is fifteen dollars. A discussion will be had at a later date in regards to that matter."

I nodded once, turned on my heel, and hurried down the hall. I did have a meeting in three minutes, but first I had to find new panties. His little demonstration melted mine right off.

Five

Lars

My groin was relaxed for the first time all day. After spending a quality ten minutes with The Diamondback, the roaring in my veins had lessened to a dull ache, but that was about to change again.

I rapped on the door to her apartment and waited. When she did not answer immediately, I pressed my lips to the door. "Miss Matthews, I can hear you breathing on the other side of the door."

The latch clicked, and she stuck her head out. "Miss Matthews? Did I do something to rub you the wrong way, boss?"

Mmm, this woman. I spent the entire day biting my tongue to avoid inappropriate responses. It looked like that was about to continue. If this were a perfect world, I would push the door open, throw her on the bed, tell her the problem was she hadn't rubbed me today, and then relieve that ache that had once again become a burn the moment I saw her.

"On the contrary, I was practicing for this evening."

"Practicing for this evening, why? Did I miss a meeting?"

The door swung open to reveal the object of my desire ... wearing a tank top and the shortest shorts I had ever the pleasure to see. Considering I was in Miami, that was saying a lot. I cleared my throat to avoid my voice sounding like that of a prepubescent boy when I spoke. "Dinner."

She shook her head at me. "We don't have a dinner scheduled for tonight. This was the one night all week that we didn't have a scheduled dinner." The way she put emphasis on the word *scheduled* told me she was indeed unhappy. I could change her mind.

I stepped into her apartment and closed the door behind me. She had definitely made the place her own since she moved in. I loved her eclectic collections ranging from flowered teacups to tiny deer figurines. I ran my hand over the open lid of her stereo cabinet. "This is new."

"Hardly. It's from the early 1970s," Serenity said, leaning against the back of a chair.

I did not take my eyes from the stereo when I spoke. "I meant to your apartment. It is incredible to see a piece like this in such pristine condition. It is more incredible to see one that opens from the top with the original player still inside. Truly magnificent. How did you come by it?"

"Do you mean how did my homeless butt manage to afford an antique? That's what you're really asking, right?"

When I glanced up, our gazes locked. I had my hands wrapped around her upper arms before she could take another breath. "I do not recall saying anything about your homeless butt or your ability to afford antiques. You are the one who said such nonsense. Do not imply that is something I would say."

Her bluster fell away, and she dropped her arms to her sides. "You're right. I'm sorry. That's all me." She rubbed her forehead in the cutest display of frustration I had ever seen. I lowered her hand back to her side without letting it go.

"Now then, how did you acquire such a lovely piece of furniture?"

She sighed heavily in resignation. "I was visiting Babette the other day, and she had it by the side of the garage for the thrift shop to pick up. I asked her if I could have it. I intended to repurpose it, but when I got it home, I discovered the player still worked, and look," she stepped around me and opened the small door on the front. Inside was a row of vinyl records. "Original albums from some of the great hitmakers of the 70s."

I knelt and pulled one out. "Wow, I do not know a lot about American music from that era, but even I know Steely Dan and The Eagles."

She motioned at them. "I know, right? I was blown away. I guess what they say is true, one man's trash is another man's treasure."

I stood and brushed off my hands. "Or in this case, woman's, but yes. It appears to be very much true. I would like to come over some night with a bottle of wine and listen to these albums. Would that be something I could impose upon you?"

She brushed her hand at me and grinned, before ducking her head. "You're never imposing. I'd love to have someone else appreciate it as much as I do. I like to put a record on, open the patio door, and sit outside on the balcony. It's relaxing at the end of a long day."

"Sounds lovely. So lovely, I might reconsider our plans."

She lifted one perfectly plucked brow at me. "Our plans? We didn't have plans. I had plans. I planned to listen to some music while sipping a Bartles & Jaymes."

"A what now?" I asked, her words foreign to my ears.

She lowered her brow in surprise. "Wait, you've never had a Bartles & Jaymes?"

"I do not recall anything by that name. I am unclear what a Bartles & Jaymes is."

She rolled her eyes and shook her head. "It's a wine cooler. Back in the '80s, they were sweet, tasty, and cheap. You know, Bartles did all the talking and ended the commercials with, *and thank you for your support.* Is this ringing any bells?"

I cracked a smile. Not at her words, but at the way she tried to imitate the guy's voice. "No, I am afraid it does not. I was all of a year old at the end of the '80s, so there is that, as you say here." I flicked my hand at her body. "You were not even born yet. How do you know about alcohol from the '80s?"

She rolled her eyes heavenward and tromped past me, but I grasped her elbow so she could not escape.

"You don't know much, do you? In America, everything from the '80s comes back around at some point to be new again. Things like My Little Pony, clear Pepsi, leggings, parachute pants, Smurfs, Tab—"

She paused for a breath, and I jumped in. "I have to say, of all the things you mentioned, I can understand why leggings came back around again. I do enjoy your little leggings."

She huffed at me and yanked her arm free. "Why are you here again? You said something about dinner. It's almost nine."

I waved my hand at her, my watch catching the setting sun through the patio door. "No, I was going to ask if you wanted to go to dinner, but I like your plans better. We should stay in, listen to music, and drink the Bartles."

"We?" she asked, her hand on her hip. "Like as in together?"

"When I went to school, that was the definition of we, yes."

She shook her head and threw up her hands. "Fine, okay, you know what? Fine. Let's listen to music and drink the Bartles."

"Should we do the pizza thing, too?"

"By pizza thing, do you mean picking up the phone and having it delivered? That feels like a lot of work."

"To use the phone?"

"To go down to the lobby and get it," she teased, heading to the kitchen.

"I can afford to pay someone to bring it to the door."

She grabbed the handle of the fridge and spun back toward me. "But why when I can have a hot *flammkuchen* on the table in thirty minutes?"

I moaned against my will. "Do not mess with my taste buds, *frau*."

She held up both hands. "I'm not messing with anything. I have everything I need to make one. I love it."

I stalked toward her and pressed her up against the door. "Why is this the first time I have heard about your ability to make German pizza?"

"Maybe because you never asked?" she squeaked, pushing against my chest to ease me back a step.

I took a moment to soak in the sight of her wearing the thin tank top in the cold room. "It seems you have many hidden talents, my *blauer vogel* chef. I cannot wait to discover them all."

The look of equal parts heat and terror that crossed her face told me exactly what I wanted to know. She was as hot for me as I was for her.

Six

Serenity

He leaned back in his chair, the warm breeze blowing across the balcony and ruffling his hair. This was probably the first time I had seen him completely and utterly relaxed since I started working here. Wound up tighter than a drum was his natural state of being, so it was nice to see him unwind and enjoy life a little bit.

"I have not had *flammkuchen* like that since …" he paused for a moment and looked to the sky, "ever. I do not know what you did with it, but it was better than any I have eaten."

I didn't want to smile, but I couldn't stop it from spreading across my face. "Thank you. It was probably the homemade sour cream and the muenster cheese. Oh," I snapped my fingers and pointed at him, "and the center-cut bacon. Less fat on the strip makes for a smokier taste to the *flammkuchen*."

"You definitely have the knack for it. Not everyone does. Where did you learn?"

To avoid answering his question, I pointed at his glass. "What do you think of the Bartles & Jaymes?"

He lifted it and turned it twice. "Also unlike anything I have ever had."

"And you don't want again?" I asked, laughing at his expression.

"I am not usually a fan of watermelon and mint. It is not bad, but I still prefer a nice bottle of wine."

I lifted my glass and tipped it at him before I took a drink. "Don't we all? The difference is, this is a heck of a lot cheaper."

He lowered his glass and leaned forward onto his knees. "Do I not pay you enough to afford a bottle of wine, Serenity? Need we reassess your contract?"

I shook my head at him. "As if, Lars. I don't have anything to spend my salary on as it is. I can afford a bottle of wine. I have several if you'd like to open one. I drink this occasionally to remind myself that happiness can be found anywhere and that my life will always be more Bartles & Jaymes than expensive bottles of wine." There was silence from the stereo for a moment until a new song started. Alabama singing *Fire in the Night*. There was always fire in the night when Lars was around.

"Why is that, Serenity?"

He leaned back in his chair again and waited for me to spill my guts. It wasn't going to happen. "I think we both already know the answer to that. There's no need to drag it up into the light of day again."

His hand reached toward the giant moon overhead. It glowed so brightly I swear it felt like I could take a step off my balcony and land right on it. Too bad that wasn't the case. I could stand to get away from this conversation.

"There is only darkness right now. It is safe to tell me those things when the darkness surrounds us."

"You already know, so why are you bringing this up now? What does it matter?"

"I know some of it, yes, but I do not know all of it. Tell me about the parts I am missing. Fill in the blanks."

I grasped my glass in my hand and leaned back in the chair, staring out over the balcony. "You know the part about my father being a German dignitary and my mother being an American actress, right?"

"I do, yes. From there, things become cloudy."

I broke eye contact and stared over his shoulder. I had to do this without sounding bitter, emotionally broken, or like I felt sorry for myself. The reality was, I often felt all three of those things. "Not much to understand. My father was killed in a car bombing when I was twelve."

"I'm sorry. That had to have been terribly difficult."

I nodded, refusing to let my chin tremble at the mere thought of it. "It was an awful age to lose a father, but I know I'm not alone. A lot of kids lose their fathers, and I remind myself I'm not special or different."

"Except for the car bombing part. Was it politically motivated?"

I held my hands out. "Probably. Let's face it, German dignitaries, whether from the '40s or the '90s, weren't exactly trusted. Regardless, he was gone. My mother and I were vacationing here when he died."

"Was your mother from Florida?"

"Yep. Right here in Miami. She just faded away after he died."

"Faded away?"

I made the motion of smoke in the air with my hand. "Faded away. My parents were soulmates, and losing him was too much for her. My mother died of a broken heart within six months of his death."

His brows didn't go up in surprise. A look crossed his face and I wondered what it meant, but he quickly shuttered his eyes before I could see more of his secrets. "I knew she had passed, but not how."

"I was barely thirteen, and suddenly, both of my parents were gone. I moved in with my American grandmother and lived with her until she died when I was fifteen. The rest is history."

He leaned on his elbow, propping his hand under his chin. "There is a lot of history in nine years, Serenity."

I took a long swallow of the cold wine cooler without answering. The music had ended, and I held up my finger, wandering back into the darkened apartment to change the record. I decided a little easy listening was in order and put on an old Nat King Cole record. I grabbed a bottle of wine and two glasses then returned to the patio. He hadn't moved, but I could feel his gaze on me the entire time. He was enjoying the tank top and boy shorts I wore, but I refused to change. A little part of me was thrilled that he found me alluring and sexy. The biggest part of me, however, was scared to death that his Big Bad Wolf might come out to play.

I lowered the wine to the table and handed him the bottle opener to uncork it. He worked at the cork carefully and waited silently. It was a skill of his that drove me a lot crazy. I was one who liked to fill empty silence out of uncomfortableness. He wanted to create the uncomfortableness out of the empty silence so you would tell him your secrets.

He poured the wine, the only sound to break the silence, and handed me the first glass. I swallowed it in one gulp. I was holding it out for a refill by the time he finished pouring his own. He refilled my glass and lowered the bottle back to the table.

"You were saying that at fifteen your grandmother died." He brought the glass to his lips as though he was the most innocent fellow in all the land. I knew the truth. He enjoyed stirring things up.

"That was where the story ended. The rest is depression and hardship, but all's well that ends well, as they say here."

He motioned around in the air with his wine glass. "*Das ist quatsch.*"

I rolled my eyes. "Call bullshit all you want, it's the truth. I had some rough years, but in the end, I graduated with a degree and landed a decent job, if I do say so myself."

He tipped his glass again and took another drink. "You lucked out when you met the professor. I'm glad he was there to make sure you were successful."

I was off the chair and in his face before I had the conscious thought to do so. "Listen here, *Mr. I was Born with a Gold Spoon in my Mouth*. I was successful because I worked my butt off for years! I was successful because I wasn't going to let the naysayers and newspapers get the best of me! I was successful because I didn't take *quatsch* from anyone, especially not *pompös* playboys who think they're better than everyone else. Maynard and Babette offered me stability, but let me assure you, even if they hadn't, I'd still be standing here with a degree in my hand working for your desperate backside!"

The smile he wore after my little tirade angered me even more. I lowered myself back to my chair with as much dignity as I could muster.

"Now, there is the German side of your *persönlichkeit*."

"If you were smart, you'd leave my German personality out of it. As you see, I tend to lose myself when it comes out to play."

He sipped his wine and stared out over the balcony. "What I saw was passion. What I saw was what I was trying to draw out with my questions. You are excellent at what you do, but you spend a lot of time holding back your true feelings about everything from business to personal matters."

I curled my legs up under me on the chair. "I still apologize for calling you desperate. You weren't, and I know that. I don't want you to think I don't appreciate the job and the benefits."

He laughed then, relaxed and happy, as though the wine had finally filtered to his brain. "You were not wrong. My butt was desperate. America, for all its wildness, has a problem talking openly about sex and self-pleasuring. I did not know if I would find someone who could do the job here or not. I needed someone who was as equally desperate for a stable position as I was for a stable hand at the helm. Hopefully, we both continue to benefit from this arrangement."

The demonstration in the display room popped into my head, and I lowered my feet to the floor. "Speaking of benefiting. Let's talk about those pictures on your app for the *neu spielzeug*."

To his credit, he never looked away or broke eye contact. "New toy? No, dear Serenity. That is not a new toy. That is a piece of finely crafted German engineering that will bring every man who owns one to their knees. I should know. Thirty minutes before I knocked on your door, I was on my knees."

I swallowed, hard, but motioned my hand at him in fake confidence. "Blah, blah, whatever. You missed my point."

"Not at all."

This man. I swear to God …

Dial it back, Serenity. You need this job, whether you want him to think you don't or not. You do. You have no place to go and no backup plan, so unless you want to be getting your ass pinched at the local cocktail bar, you'd better channel some yin.

That didn't mean I was taking it lying down, though.

"My pictures. Your phone. Why?"

He blew a breath through his lips, and it was the first time I had ever seen him slightly flustered about anything. "I told you, the app allows the user to add videos and pictures to watch while the aid is in use. Some men use *erotisch* … err … a sexy video of their lover?" I nodded, and he continued. "Others may use images to heighten their experience, while others may use nothing at all."

I pursed my lips and wiggled them around. "Nope, I still didn't hear an actual explanation of why my pictures were on your app."

He shook his head in frustration. "Serenity, it was for demonstration purposes only."

"Didn't feel that way to me, Lars. In fact, you could have used any scantily clad adult entertainment actress for demonstration purposes only. Instead, you had pictures of me. They weren't even sensual pictures. They were just me doing everyday things. Your reaction told me it was a lot more than a demonstration."

"That reminds me," he said, his long, erotic fingers setting the glass back on the table, "we need to talk about your fifteen-dollar garbage aid versus a Kontakt aid."

I snorted and shook my head. "Not until we finish talking about why you're using my picture to jack off to."

He gagged, and for a split second, I thought he was going to vomit. He spun in his chair to face me and grasped my chin. "Never repeat those words. Vulgarity has no place within the confines of Kontakt."

It took me a moment to sort out what words I wasn't supposed to say. "Uh, what am I supposed to call it then? That's what we call it here."

"Maybe in the adult entertainment crowd."

I laughed with sarcasm. "No, pretty much every crowd, Lars."

"In this crowd," he said, making a circle around us and the building, "we will call it what it is."

"Which is?"

"Self-pleasuring."

I pinned him with a stare, but he didn't break eye contact. Finally, I held up my hands in defeat. "Alright, fine. Why were you using my photos during self-pleasure? But wait. Can you call it self-pleasuring when you're using the aid?"

"As long as you are alone," he answered, clearly exasperated.

"That was the answer to the latter. How about the former?"

Honest to God, Lars Jäger rolled his eyes at me. I never expected the CEO of a sex toy company to roll his eyes at me when discussing anything to do with sex.

"If I must spell it out for you, I find you to be *der typ*."

"I'm your type? Seriously? Thanks for the laugh, Lars," I said, chuckling. "That's smashingly funny right there."

His hand still held my chin, and his eyes were laser-focused on my lips. "I am not laughing, am I?"

"You're serious?"

"As serious about this as I am about not letting you call my product a sex toy."

I managed to hold in the laughter that wanted to spill out. "You are deadly serious about that, I have to say. Still can't say I feel comfortable with the knowledge you use that app when I'm not there." I was flustered and not making any sense between his proximity and the wine I'd consumed.

"Would you feel more comfortable if you were there?" His lips were a hairsbreadth from mine. "I could arrange for that. Then I wouldn't need the app." I swallowed, and his laughter was filled with naughty victory. "For once, the little *blauer vogel* is speechless. Now I know her weakness."

His words fell away as soon as his lips brushed across mine. It wasn't so much a kiss as it was … contact. His lips were hot, wet, and tasted of wine. I whimpered at the idea that was all I would get, and the sound was the spark to his desire. The second time his lips touched mine, he didn't brush them across. He planted them firmly and let me taste the sweet wine on his lips. When he forced my lips open with his determined tongue, I tasted the smoky bacon on his. I moaned, and he wrapped his fingers in my hair to tug me closer to him, his wet tongue turning my insides into a bowl of Jell-O.

I was completely inexperienced and I didn't know what to do, so I followed my instincts. I did what I had wanted to do since the first day in his office. I slid my fingers into his hair and tightened them. The sensation was unlike any other when he had his tongue down my throat. We shared a mutual moan that echoed across the balcony into the dark night. I had never heard of anyone having an orgasm from a kiss, but I was damn close just thinking about what it would feel like to have more than his tongue inside me.

With practiced ease, he let his lips fall away, going back twice for a short peck before he rested his forehead on mine. His intense blue eyes were deep and smoky when he spoke. "I heard your answer in that moan, dear Serenity. You would definitely like to be there," he whispered before he lowered his lips again.

Seven

Serenity

I stood in the elevator and ran my fingers over my lips. They were still there. I had checked frequently the last two days to be sure Lars hadn't singed them off with those kisses. Thank God he didn't know that was my first kiss. How embarrassing would that have been? At least when he kissed me for twenty minutes with his hands wrapped in my hair, his tongue down my throat, and a giant erection in his pants, I knew they weren't pity kisses. He absolutely wanted to be kissing me. I absolutely turned him on. Not bad for a beginner.

Seducing Serenity

The door chimed its prim and positively perfect ding then slid open to reveal the inner sanctum. Since the kiss, he'd managed to avoid me for the better part of two days. He talked to me only during meetings or in public areas. When he did, his gaze was focused on my lips, which I made sure always wore a coat of shiny gloss. I had to chuckle at how he acted like he was sixteen instead of thirty.

"Serenity!" Lexie called from the copy room, motioning me in.

"Hey, Lexie," I said, a spring in my step and a happy tone to my voice.

Why, you ask? Wasn't it obvious? A guy like Lars Jäger had the hots for me! Never, in all my life, did I think that could happen. I'm a twenty-four-year-old virgin, and he's a thirty-year-old CEO of a sensual aid company. Talk about opposites attracting. "How's your morning?"

"Not so good," she whispered as soon as I was standing next to her.

"I'm sorry, did something happen?" I noticed the papers she was collating and tipped my head. "Why are you putting together third-quarter financials?"

"She's going to want to see them."

"She? She who?" I asked, confused by her fear and anxiety so early in the morning.

"Gretchen Jäger. She arrives tonight. He didn't tell you?" she whispered in a comical stage whisper.

"Is. He. In?" I asked in a tone that said all it needed to.

"His office." She turned back to the copier while I spun on my heel and stomped down the hallway.

I threw the door open and stomped in, slamming it behind me. "Why didn't you tell me your mother is coming tonight!"

He glanced up from his computer and straightened his tie. "Was that a question? It sounded more like an angry statement."

"Lexie just told me Gretchen Jäger is flying in tonight. Is that or is that not your mother?"

"She is definitely my *mutter,* according to my birth certificate."

I threw my arms out wide. "And you didn't think it was important for me to know that she was coming?"

"I was going to tell you this morning."

"This morning! This morning! Gee, thanks for the advanced notice. Why didn't you tell me sooner?"

He motioned at me with both hands. "I need not say more."

My shoulders deflated, and I fell into the chair opposite his desk. "Wait. Why is your mother coming, and why does she need to see third-quarter financials?"

He leaned back and steepled his fingers together. "She owns the business."

"You're her son. Doesn't she trust you?"

"She does, but you have not met my *mutter*. She has a hand in every part of this business, and that will not change until the day she no longer draws a breath. She wants to meet the people I have hired and talk to them about their vision for her company. She is not an ogre to fear, Serenity. She is not interested in presentations and flowcharts. She wants to sit down and talk to you over dinner about what you see as our strengths and weaknesses. Take a deep breath and relax. She has already seen the financials, of course. Lexie is simply running off copies for everyone. We will discuss them together and find ways to improve our bottom line."

I sucked in a deep breath and held it before I let it back out. "Okay, I'm sorry for overreacting. Gretchen is so," I motioned around with my hands, "important, and I'm so not important. I don't want to do or say something that will put me out of a job."

He stood and came around the desk, resting his butt on it and swinging his leather-clad heel against it. "She is no more important than you are. We all play a role in this company. If you are not here working your magic to sell the product, we do not have a company."

I tossed my hand out to the side. "Sure you would. You'd just hire someone else. I mean, let's face it, I'm replaceable, she's not."

"We are all replaceable if we go at it from that angle, Serenity. It is not about being replaced. I know you struggle with that concept because of your childhood, but she wants the U.S. division of the company to succeed. She will give us anything and do anything we need her to do to ensure that. Deep breath. No one is getting fired. I happen to know that she is already happy with where we are. We are turning a profit early when we should still be in the spending phase. That profit is due to you and your skills, do not underestimate your importance here."

"I've never been good at that."

He finally cracked a smile and winked at me. His long lashes brushed his cheek in a way that made me more than a little hot under the collar. It made me burn bright with desire. "I had no idea it was not your strong suit. You are always so confident."

"Wow, Lars Jäger knows sarcasm. I'm impressed," I teased, brushing off my pencil skirt.

"Lars Jäger knows a lot that you would be impressed with. Until he can show you those things, he wants you to know that the owner of this company will be arriving at midnight to Miami International. You will not have to meet with her until tomorrow early evening. Due to the time change, she will be going to bed about the time you get up. You will have plenty of time to prepare for the meeting. I have her scheduled in blocks to meet with other people in the building throughout the afternoon, but you do not need to worry yourself with that. The three of us will sit down here in my office around six to go over everything closely and then have a private dinner in my penthouse directly after. Acceptable?"

I nodded once. It didn't matter if it was acceptable. He was paying me to be available at any and all times. He was asking as a matter of manners, but he expected no answer other than yes. "I'll be ready. That gives me time to buy a power suit. I'll need it to hold my own with someone like your mother."

He propped himself on the arms of my chair and held my eyes. "Darling, you do not need a power suit to hold your own. You hold your own against me every single day. If you can do that, you have nothing to fear from her. Confidence, remember?"

His lips came down on mine again, and he kissed me with far less tongue and for far less time than I had hoped. When he stood up again, he licked his lips, making me whimper. I had to start carrying panties around in my purse. I was tired of running back to my apartment to change them every time his kisses made my lower half dewy.

"What does your day look like today?" he asked, slipping back around to bring up his calendar.

I cleared my throat before I spoke, so I didn't sound needy. "I have a meeting in twenty minutes with Seth about the café. We also have our potential client meeting at two p.m. Why?"

"After our meeting this afternoon, I have a field trip planned." He motioned at my bag where my phone was. "Mark yourself as out after the meeting. We will have dinner when we are done."

I raised my head from typing into my phone. "A field trip? Where are we going? The zoo?"

"Some might call it that, but no, not technically. You will find out when we get there. In the meantime, I expect a full briefing about the café before our next meeting."

"You could come with me. We have no secrets."

He gave me a smile that said he was amused. "I would, but I have about thirty other things I would rather be doing. Number one on my list is something not suitable for work." His gaze swept from my heels to the hem of my skirt and stopped.

I jumped up and hot-footed it to the door. "Right, okay, no problem. See you soon."

When I shut the door behind me, I swear to God I could hear him laughing.

"Serenity? Earth to Serenity," Seth said, waving his hand in front of my face.

I snapped to attention and smiled. "Sorry, I got distracted for a second there."

"For a second? You've been distracted since you got here. Does it have anything to do with the German CEO in the penthouse?"

"He's not in the penthouse. He's in his office." I rolled my eyes until I realized what I had said. I slapped my hand over my mouth. "Crap. I didn't mean it like that."

It was his turn to roll his eyes. "Sure, and my chihuahua wasn't eaten by a gator."

My head snapped in his direction. "It was?"

He grimaced and nodded. "Never saw it coming. Anyway, what has the ol' boss man done to distract you this time?"

I wasn't about to tell him he stuck his tongue down my throat … again. I brushed my hand at him nonchalantly as we entered the café. "No big deal. He forgot to tell me his mother was coming in tonight, but that's fine. It's time we meet her, don't you think?"

He nodded while he flipped on the lights. "I think so. Everyone has made her out to be Brunhilda. I think we all need a reset on who she is and what she expects out of this side of the company. Now, that's easy for me to say, all I have to do is keep the building running. You, on the other hand, have to sell those expensive vibrators and keep it classy."

I was taking a drink of coffee and snorted it right up my sinus cavities and back out again. I bent over, coffee dripping down my face, and laughter choking out my voice. Seth handed me a napkin, and I cleaned myself up, the whole time unsure if I should be laughing or grumping about his comments.

"Thanks, Seth. I appreciate the dry-cleaning bill."

"Anytime." He smiled slyly. "I'm sure you could run upstairs and change in the boss's office. He might turn his back."

I put my hand on my hip and stared him down. "Are you trying to say something here, Seth?"

He pointed at his chest while mouthing, *me?*

I shoved him in the shoulder and tossed my bag down on a table. "Yes, you. Clearly, you think you know something you don't know."

He held up his hands. "I don't know anything, we all know that. I'm joking around … mostly. We'd all have to be blind not to notice the way he looks at you when he thinks no one else is, though."

"And how does he look at me when no one else is looking? Disappointed? Unsure?

Like prey?" I threw the last one in to test the waters.

"Revered. Everyone is in agreement on that word, too, so stop turning up your lip in disbelief," he said, swirling his finger around my face.

"Good Lord, who else are you discussing this with?"

He hooked his arm in mine and led me toward the café kitchen. "Let's see … um … oh, everyone," he teased, shoulder bumping me. "If he thinks he's hiding his emotions, he's wrong. If you think we can't see you're scared to death of his prowess, you're wrong. I know you don't like being wrong, so my guess is you have this all locked down."

If only he knew how not locked down I had this.

"Sure, yeah, it's locked down tight."

He laughed until he had to drop my arm and wipe his eyes. "That was convincing. Never hesitate and never show weakness, Serenity. Especially not to a guy like Lars."

I laughed hysterically, but dryly, to tell him I wasn't playing this game any longer. "Clearly, you think there is something there that isn't. We work together, end of story. Speaking of, we have to do something with this place. We signed the caterers for ninety days. That time has passed, but we still need an open and successful café.

"Smooth change of subject, boss," he said, laughing.

"I'm not your boss, not by a long shot. We are equals in this business, Seth. I can't do my job if you aren't doing yours and vice versa." The little lesson Lars schooled me on in his office came back to me. I sighed when it struck me that he'd managed to make his point without even being present. "Let's work together to get the job done. We already know the café is a popular place for our colleagues. Do you think we could draw in business from the other office buildings to make it self-sufficient? We have to take wages and product into consideration, too."

He motioned me to the counter where two books lay open and waiting. "These are the reports from the caterers for the ninety days they were here. It was only three months, so we don't have a lot of data, but even after we paid out their contract, we were in the black by thousands. Since I run the reception desk, I can tell you we had several groups coming over for lunch every day from three different buildings. There are no other cafes on this end of the district, so unless you want to have it delivered, you're brown-bagging it. Last week, I had a group come in for coffee and pastries with a potential client who was tight on time between flights."

I leaned on the counter and crossed my arms over my chest. "You're saying the outside revenue is already coming in."

"To a degree, yes. Most of the traffic is over lunch, though. With a little bit of marketing on your end, we could have the place filled throughout the day. I don't think that would be a problem. What is the problem? Staffing. I don't know anything about hiring people to run a café."

I held up my finger. "You don't have to. That's a human resource problem. All we do is tell them what we need, and they hire the positions, starting with a manager. Then we sit down with the manager and go over our ideas and what our marketing directive is. I know this is kind of your baby, so you can have as much or as little say in it as you want, but don't even think about wanting to run it. We wouldn't survive without you at the helm of this building."

He grinned and patted my shoulder. "Thanks for saying so, but you could always hire three other people to replace me."

I winked and pointed at him. "You almost had me." I turned and took in the space. "I like how the café butts up to the courtyard. We could put a few tables out on the patio where people could sit and enjoy the gardens. What would you think of calling it Kontakt Café?"

He made the mind blown motion with his hand. "Wow. You just blew me away with that marketing genius name. I didn't see it coming."

I stuck my tongue out at him while he laughed. "Hear me out. Do you remember the movie Contact with Jodie Foster?" He nodded, but I could see the confusion in his eyes. "What if we made the logo for the café a satellite? We would put it on the to-go cups and food packaging. Subtle, but it would be an instant association for people. We would spell it the same as the company, but people won't have a hard time remembering the name. Who cares if they spell it C O N T A C T as long as they utilize the café?"

He shook his finger at me. "I get what you're saying now. Are we going to have a dildo sticking out of the center of the satellite?"

My laughter filled the café until I couldn't breathe. I had to bend over and suck in air like a four-pack-a-day smoker. "Oh. My. God. I can't believe you said that. First of all, it's a sensual aid."

He was wiping tears from his eyes, and a new round started at my comment. Finally, he held his hand up and waved it. "I'm sorry. A sensual aid sticking out the center of it."

"The answer is no. We will pretend to keep it classy, and no one will be the wiser."

"I'm not following. How do you pretend to keep it classy?" Seth asked, absolutely perplexed.

"You name the products and drinks on the menu after items in your sensual aids catalog."

He chewed on his lip while a sneaky grin lifted the corners. "I knew there was a reason

I liked you. Subliminal messaging while keeping marketing simple."

I tipped my head to the left in agreement. "I'll give you a little bit of insider information. Bring back the hot dog wrapped in pizza dough and name it The Diamondback."

"Diamondback? Like the snake? We don't have anything in the catalog named that."

"Yet. You're going to want to be on the list to test it when it becomes available, and I'm not talking about the hot dog." I winked, and that small smile he wore grew into a full-fledged grin.

Eight

Lars

I was slowly losing it. I never saw her coming. When she hit me with that smile the first time, I was a goner, and I did not even know it. She was all that and a bag of chips, as they say here. I knew I had to have her after that kiss the other night. After the one this morning, I was aware I had crossed a line I could not uncross. If she wanted to, she had me dead to rights for kissing her in my office. My penthouse or her apartment was a different story, but doing it right in the place her contract says it would never happen was *blöd*. That kind of stupidity could land the whole company in hot water. I had to remember to be more careful about when and where I touched her. Let there be no doubt. I would touch her again. I would kiss her. I would, one day, make love to her. I just had to remember to do it in a place that would not break any contract rules.

On the ride down to the lobby, my hand was at her back, and her heat soaked into my palm. I should stay hands-off, but to a casual observer, it looked like nothing more than me helping her over the elevator threshold when the doors opened. To me, it was scratching an itch. I had needed to touch her since she walked out of my office hours ago.

"Where are we going?" she asked again. She had been asking since I told her to change into something for fun and … pleasure.

"Patience, my little—"

"I am not a blue bird!" she exclaimed, throwing her hands up in the air.

"You are also not patient," I said, a smile on my lips when I passed Seth, who held the door for us. "Thanks, Seth. We'll be back, but do not wait up for us."

"You got it, boss," he said, letting the door close behind us.

"My car or you—"

I beeped the horn on mine and opened the door for her to sit.

"Well, hello yours," she said, settling into the buttery leather seat.

"Mine is a convertible. We are young, free, and good looking. We should show the world."

She threw her head back on the headrest and laughed. I put it in gear and spun out of the parking lot onto the service road. I turned left onto North Miami Avenue, and she threw her hands up while her hair flew around her face. Her laughter filled my head, and it hit me square in the gut how she was so much more than I saw that first day. To have gone through what she had gone through and still be able to enjoy life was a definite plus mark on the side of humanity.

Maybe it canceled out my cynical side of humanity. I did not bounce back the way she did. I cannot laugh with abandon or throw my hands up in the air to enjoy the simple pleasure of the wind in my hair. I would study Serenity and hope she would teach me about living life the way it was meant to be lived, completely, and without regard for tomorrow.

She tapped me on the shoulder, and I flicked my eyes to her for a moment as I slowed for a light. "You're lost in thought. Are you okay?"

I smiled and came to a complete stop. "Of course. I still have to concentrate on where I am going since I have not lived here long."

"If you'd share the destination, I might be able to help with the navigating," she said pointedly.

"What fun would that be?" I asked and slammed my foot down on the accelerator as soon as the light turned green.

She squealed, but it quickly turned to laughter. The sun was already setting, and *Mutter* would be here in a few hours, but this had to be done before she arrived. Not only for Serenity but for me. I slowed for a right turn and motored toward my destination, searching for a parking spot.

She tugged on my sleeve. "This isn't a great part of town, Lars. We shouldn't leave the car parked out here on the street. What are we doing down here anyway?"

I maneuvered the car into a spot at the curb and cut the engine, hitting the button to raise the convertible top. It wouldn't deter thieves, but it would stop seagulls from pooping on my leather seats. "The car has an alarm and a locked steering wheel. No one is going to drive away with it. If they can figure out a way, more power to them," I said, releasing my safety belt.

"Wait," she grabbed my shirt sleeve, "are we going to Steely Dan's?" Her sarcastic laughter was evident inside the now enclosed car.

"We are."

"You know that Steely Dan's is a sex shop, right?"

I nodded once. "I am aware, but I do have a question. Why does everyone here call themselves Steely Dan? Is that some kind of manly man name?"

She waved her hand in the *hold up* motion. "You don't know what Steely Dan is?"

"It is a band, is it not?"

"It is, but where did the band get the name from?"

"I have not the faintest clue."

She sucked in a breath and closed her eyes, holding her hands to her chest in harmony. "Don't mind me. I'm enjoying the fact that I know something about sex that you don't. Give me a moment to revel in it, please."

"Your moment is up," I said sarcastically.

Her eyes popped open and she turned to me. "Steely Dan was the name of a steam-powered dildo from the book Naked Lunch by William Burroughs. The full name was Steely Dan III from Yokohama. I can't believe you didn't know that considering the business you're in."

"I have questions," I said, ignoring her barb. "Why would you want to be named after a dildo, and why would you need a steam-powered one?"

She smacked herself in the forehead with the palm of her hand. "You have to be the biggest joy kill in the whole of the U.S. and Germany." She patted my chest the way a mother would a child. "Just enjoy the story and stop overanalyzing it."

I rubbed my jaw while I stared into her beautiful eyes. "We should name our next sensual aid Steely Dan. We could use stainless steel and give it a real industrial feel. Do you think it would sell?"

She rolled her eyes to the roof of the car. "I could sell that to a wide swath of the population without even trying. Add some diamond plating on the handle, and you've got a winner."

I clapped my hands once and laughed. "Well, well, my little *blauer vogel* is learning her lessons well! I do believe we have our first collaborative sensual aid. This will be our project. Just you and me making all the decisions, and ..." I paused for effect, "testing."

Her long and hard swallow told me the idea of how mind-blowing that testing could be had just crossed her mind. "Sure," she squeaked before clearing her throat, "anything to further the company. Is that why we're here? Checking out the competition?"

I opened my door and swiveled my legs out. "Hardly." I waved my hand at the run-down building. "There is no competition here, but they will have that fifteen-dollar aid you insist is better than a Kontakt aid." Before she could say anything more, I exited the car and jogged around to her side. I opened the door for her, and she remained in her seat, her arms folded across her chest with her jaw clenched together. "Serenity, are you coming?"

"No, I'm not. I'm not coming now or anytime in the future with either a fifteen-dollar vibrator or a fifteen-thousand-dollar vibrator."

I leaned on the doorframe to angle in closer to her. "You are coming ... into the store. What happens in private is none of my business. Well, it is my business, but one step at a time. You were the one to start this, and now it is up to you to prove yourself right and me wrong."

As expected, that got her moving. She unbuckled her belt and climbed out of the car in a huff. "Oh, don't worry, I can prove you wrong in a heartbeat. Steely Dan's is full of cheap vibrators. While we're here, we should get you one of those low budget canister strokers. They don't use an app. If you want a video, you better find yourself some free porn."

She breezed past me and I let her go. I had to breathe in deeply a few times and force my spine straight, so I did not fall to my knees. Her comment about not coming was making it challenging to stay appropriate. I wanted to say I could make her come without a sensual aid, but my *mutter's* disapproving face loomed in my vision the instant I thought of it. Better to hold my tongue than lose my job. Images reeled through my mind of what my tongue could do to make her come. I groaned, shaking my arms out after I let the door close behind me. The store was dark, and I put a protective hand to her back.

"This place definitely says *schäbig*," I whispered. From what I could see, we were the only ones here. Then I noticed a curtain covered door at the back that smacked of private viewing rooms.

"Oh, it's definitely seedy, but you're the one who insisted we come," she said haughtily. "Would you like to leave?"

"Not until we have what we came for," I replied casually, stopping next to a display.

I caught a red flash out of the corner of my eye and broke away from her, staring at a display of giant, red, jelly penises. I wrapped my fingers around one and flopped it back and forth in a strange show of sexual deviance. Waving it brought out the scent, which was fake strawberries overlaid on cheap plastic. It had to be over a foot long and so thick my thumb and forefinger did not touch where I grasped it.

"*Was zur Hölle?*" I muttered at the thing while it quivered in my hand.

"What the hell, Lars?" she hissed, coming up behind me.

"That is what I want to know," I agreed, waiting for her to answer.

"I mean, what the hell are you doing?"

She was plastered the length of me, and I had to admit I liked it way too much. Her curves wrapped around my arm, belly, hip, and thigh like a second skin. I just got a hard-on in a sex shop thinking about this woman being wrapped around me naked. I glanced down right into her beautiful eyes and swallowed back a moan that wanted to escape. *Verdammt*! She was the sexiest thing in this shop, and she did not even know it.

I gave my wrist a flick and the jelly dong flopped back and forth again. "What is this?"

She snatched it from my hand and set it back on the shelf where it wiggled and jiggled from the balls up. "It's a Herbert Horsecock," she whisper-hissed. "Don't touch things."

"What is a Herbert Horsecock?" My tongue was thick in my mouth when my eyes caught a glimpse of her perfect cleavage. She was tiny, but her chest was not, and it was all I would ever need in this life.

"Isn't it self-explanatory?" she asked, her eyes rolling around in her head. "It's a big, rubber," she glanced around and leaned in close to my ear, "*schwanz*."

I let out a soft snort. "Did you just use the German word for dong, so you did not have to say it? It is okay, Serenity. Are you saying it is a big rubber dong?"

"Shh," she whispered immediately. "Shouldn't you already know what it is? You run one of these companies for heaven's sake!"

I bit my tongue, so laughter did not spill out. Something told me laughing would be a terrible idea. Maybe it was the way her eyes shot daggers at me when she stared me down. "Sugar pie, we do not have, what did you call it? A Herbert Horsecock? We do not have those in our catalog and never will. I do believe those are uniquely American. Everything is bigger and better in America, no?"

"In this case, it's definitely bigger," she agreed. "I don't know about better, though. It looks like it would hurt."

We both sat staring at it and nodding our heads. "Maybe it is just for display."

"Like for decoration?"

"Sure," I agreed, turning my head left and then right, "maybe women use them for … nope … I cannot think of anything."

She let out the laugh she had been holding in, and her shoulders shook. Her hand was at her mouth to hold it in, but she failed miserably. Soon tears were running down her face. When she caught her breath, she turned and rested her forehead on my chest. "I'm glad I wasn't the only one without a good use for it."

I wrapped my arms around her without thought and held her to me. Her soft body was warm and distinctly feminine. "We should find what we came for so we can get dinner before *Mutter* arrives."

She lifted her head and shook it slightly. "We don't need anything here. I'd probably get electrocuted using one of these."

I raised one brow at her. "Suddenly, Kontakt's products are moving up in the world?"

"I never said Kontakt's products weren't quality. I said a fifteen-dollar vibrator will do the same thing a fifteen-thousand-dollar one will do." She dumped her head in her hand. "*Verdammt!*"

I grasped her hand and pulled her along behind me. "Dammit is right. You almost had me convinced to leave, but now you reminded me of your assumptions, so we stay. It should not be hard to find a fifteen-dollar vibrator here." We weaved up and down the aisles until we found the display we were looking for. I eyed the price tags and designs. "We are going to start small," I explained, my eyes searching for just the right one until I spotted it left of center. I lifted it off the hook and held it high above my head like a champion. "You cannot get closer than $14.99. Let us go check out."

She applied surprising resistance to my hand when I tried to drag her to the counter. "We are not buying that," she said between clenched teeth. "Didn't you see the sign? It says they will try each toy to make sure it works."

I spun on my heel and stared at her. "Why is this a surprise? We hand-test every Kontakt sensual aid. Once you take it home, you cannot return it," I said, shaking it slightly.

"I'm never using it, so it doesn't matter," she ground out, crossing her arms over her chest.

A smile tipped my lips, and I bounced up on my toes. "That is what you think."

I spun back around and headed to the counter. She could follow me or not, but it mattered not at all. I did not care if she used this, but she was going to use the Kontakt aid. If I had done my job right, she would then understand what sets us apart from places like this.

Nine

Serenity

The food was terrific, but I was stuffed. I set my fork down on my plate and leaned back on the couch, the pillows cushy against my tired back. It took some doing, but I convinced Lars I wasn't in the mood to eat out. We had plenty of time to grab takeout and eat at home before his mother arrived.

"Tell me about your mother. I know next to nothing other than her name and that she birthed you."

He finished chewing his last bite of Tom Yum Goong and tossed his napkin next to his plate. He picked up his wine glass and leaned back to relax, too. "She is probably unlike anyone you have ever met."

"Oh, boy," I sighed.

He waved his hand at me until he lowered his wine glass. "That is not a bad thing, Serenity. I simply meant it is not often that a single woman in Germany amasses the empire she has, in sensual aids especially. The majority of companies are run by men."

I pointed at him. "Which is ironic because you're talking about products made for women. Men don't know what women like."

"Not true. Basic aids have stayed the same, and sold consistently, for a lot of years."

I lowered my brow at him. "Honestly, Lars. How hard is it to design something that looks like the appendage already hanging off of you? It's not exactly rocket science for Pete's sake."

He laughed then, the sound full, dark, and sexy as hell. Suddenly, and inexplicably, I wanted to see his appendage. Truth be told, I wanted to do more than see it. "I will give you that point, Miss Matthews. My *mutter* was the creator of many of the new products on the market. She would design and create, and other companies copied her."

"Don't they say imitation is the sincerest form of flattery?"

He tipped his glass at me. "They do, and as you saw tonight, not all copies are Kontakt quality."

"What possessed her to start a company like this? I'm assuming she didn't take it over from someone."

"She did not. Kontakt is hers and hers alone."

"It's yours now, too."

"Not true." He lowered the glass to the table. "I am not an equal owner in Kontakt. I own stock, but I have no voting rights at the table. The company is owned solely by *Mutter*. I am the CEO of the U.S. division, but I am paid the same as the other CEO, which is her. I have no doubt if she does not like what I am doing, I am easily replaced. I may understand the business and what she wants out of us here, but I had better perform and move the company forward, or she will find someone who will."

"Wow," I breathed out, "she's hardcore. Tough as nails. Doesn't take any flak. I'm definitely afraid to meet her now. As much as I pretend I don't, I actually need this job."

He turned to me and rested his hand on my bent knee. "*Mutter* is none of those things in real life, Serenity. She cares about her business and the people who work for her. She expects a lot out of us, but she also gives us the tools we need to be successful. If we are not successful, then it is because of our own laziness. She is no tougher on me than she is on anyone else in the company. Personally, I am glad she runs the company the way she does. She is trying to survive in a man's world, and she refuses to be at the bottom of the pack. Once you meet her, you will understand that her soft, caring side overpowers her tough as nails side, though. She will do anything for anyone at any time if it is within her means."

I relaxed again, even with his hand on my knee in an oddly intimate way. "You never talk about your father, just your grandfather."

His eyes hooded and his hand started massaging my knee. I would like to say it was absently, but I had no doubt it wasn't. "*Mutter* used a sperm donor and raised me alone. She had no interest in being a wife. She wanted to be a CEO and *mutter*, nothing more, nothing less."

I'm sure my face showed surprise at his admittance. "Wow, I guess I don't know what to say about that."

"Nothing to say, Serenity. She gave me everything I needed. I was lucky to have my grandfather all the way through my impressionable years. He was my father figure, and I never once questioned why I did not have a father present at home. You will understand when you meet Gretchen. How do you say it here?" He motioned his hands around. "She handles her own business?"

I laughed then, the wine filling my head and his little cultural differences amusing.

"She handles her own shit," I clarified, and he grinned, pointing at me once. "She definitely sounds like she can handle herself. I'm excited to meet her, even if I don't sound like I am. I want her to like what we've done so far, and it's stressful to know how much the success of the company falls on me. I don't want her to think I'm a slacker."

He chuckled and brushed a piece of hair off my forehead. "*Mutter* already knows you are not a slacker. She has commented several times over the last month how insightful you are. Not only with marketing the product but with playing off sensationalism in an understated way. That might not make sense to you right now, but it will once you sit down with her. I cannot wait for you to tell her about the changes you have planned for the café. It will be obvious to her that you have your finger on the pulse of America."

I laughed and rested my cheek on the couch. "Well, that is my job, so I guess I better be good at it. I also better let you get to the airport to pick her up. She doesn't strike me as the type of woman who wants to be kept waiting."

He smiled a smile that told me I had hit the nail on the head. "You are right, but before I head out, I have something for you."

He stood and held his hand out for me to take. I grasped it, and he pulled me up off the couch and opened my front door, motioning me out. "We have to leave my apartment? Did you forget something in the office?"

He shook his head and put his hand to the small of my back, propelling me along with him until we came to a stop at the door of his penthouse. He swiped his card and held the door open for me. It wasn't the first time I had been in his private space, but it still made my breath catch every time. In the office, he was all sleek cars and well-cut suits, but not here. His home was the traditional German country cottage. His furniture was simple, understated, and welcomed you like you'd been a friend forever. Sure, it was state of the art in its technology and appliances, not to mention an out of this world jacuzzi on his balcony, but it wasn't what you would expect if you had met Lars in the boardroom. Personally, if I had a choice, I'd take the Lars who lived in that bedroom over the one in the boardroom any day. His bed filled the room nearly to capacity, but the look of it told me it would envelop you like the arms of a lover and never let you go.

I shook my head and rolled my eyes at myself. Good Lord, Serenity. You need to get a grip before the head boss lady gets here and notices the way you look at her son, who also happens to be your boss.

He closed the door behind him and motioned me toward his bedroom. I stayed put. I wasn't standing by the soft bed wrapped in satin sheets and a gingham comforter. I wasn't staring at the jacuzzi filled with bubbles and warm water, and I wasn't thinking about the things he had hidden in the stand next to his bed. I diverted to the kitchen instead and leaned against the center island.

The kitchen was rustic meets modern with old-world style cabinets, a giant farmhouse sink, and tile counters. The appliances blended into the kitchen behind doors that matched the cabinetry, but you could tell it had very little use since he moved in. This kitchen felt sad from disuse. My heart broke a little bit to think he didn't have the time, or the friends, to host the kind of parties Miami is famous for. Then again, he probably had friends, but they were still living their lives in Germany while he uprooted his life to come here. I hadn't considered how difficult that must have been for him. For all I knew, he had a lot of friends and family in Germany, and he left it all to help his mother.

"Did you have a girlfriend in Germany?" I blurted out, surprising both of us.

His head tipped the way it does when he's curious, and his hair relaxed across his forehead. "Why would you ask that?"

He braced a hand on each side of me, essentially holding me to the island. He was too close. Too virile. Too out of my league. I couldn't look away.

"It just hit me that you probably left a lot of people you cared about in Germany when you came over here. Also, there was that kissing thing. I don't want to be the whore on this side of the pond who tries to steal someone's man."

Instantly, his hand grasped my chin, and he used his hard, hot body to hold me against the island. "Use that word again about yourself and we'll have problems."

I stared into his icy blue eyes, mesmerized by their beauty and depth. This man was sex all night long. He was frantic, uncontrolled sex on the boardroom table. He was languid sex in the jacuzzi under the stars. He was everything. I was nothing compared to who and what he was.

"Note made," I squeaked, his intensity sending a tremor through me.

He noticed and relented his grip, but didn't drop his hand altogether. We were nose-to-nose when he spoke again. "I left Germany free and clear. I came here looking for a new life, Serenity. The only thing I left in Germany that I cared about was my *mutter*, everything else I was happy to leave behind. There is nothing left for me there. There is no girlfriend, family, or any friends to speak of. My life in Germany was nothing more than an empty shell of hopelessness. At the end of every day, I was still aching for a connection with someone who understood the past was sometimes painful, and moving on from it was always hard."

"And you found that here?" My voice was barely audible in the cavernous room.

"I found that in you. You cannot deny the commonality we share, Serenity."

I braced my hand on his chest, not to push him away, but to stop myself from falling into him and soaking in his heat. "I'm sorry," I whispered.

"For what? Asking an honest question and getting an honest answer?" he asked, his hand coming up to brush a piece of hair off my cheek.

My head shook with sadness. "For the way you feel. I understand the ache of that kind of pain all the way to my core. I wouldn't wish it on my worst enemy. I wish you didn't feel that way. It's a burden I would rather you didn't have to carry."

"Maybe I carry it for a reason. It has taken me years to find anyone I could connect with the way I connect with you. I do not understand it. I know it complicates our situation in the boardroom. I know it puts me at risk for a lawsuit I cannot afford. Yet, I cannot stay away from you."

His words made my heart pound, and I wanted a reason, any reason, to deny what he was saying was true. "Maybe that's because I'm younger than you are, and you think you have to protect me."

His head shook slowly, but his gaze never left mine. "Your age has nothing to do with it, Serenity. You are twenty-four going on forty-four. You are far wiser and more mature than I am at thirty. The only thing you need protection from is me."

"Parts of me aren't so mature," I whispered. "Some parts of me are far younger than my twenty-four—"

His lips crushed mine and sliced my sentence off. He slid his hands up my shoulders and neck until they grasped my face, gently tipping my head to the left while his lips massaged mine into a soft sigh. My lips parted, he darted in, and his tongue took what it had wanted all along. All of me.

He took my pain and gave me his. He took my loneliness and made it disappear. I took his loneliness and stored it away, offering him a few moments of peace. All the while, his tongue stroked mine in a dance of hunger, desire, and passion I had never experienced before. My fingers fisted his shirt, and I sighed again, the sound more like a moan to my own ears. He broke the kiss slowly and with considerable hesitation. We stood panting in his kitchen, the lights low, and desire radiating from us.

An expletive fell from his lips. "*Scheiß*! I hate this and love this all at the same time." His hand went to his hair to grasp the locks while taking a much-needed step back.

I let his tie slide through my fingers. "I'm sorry. This is my fault. I should be more …" I motioned my hands around until I finally dropped them.

"Be more what? More sexy? More alluring? More incredible? You are already all of those things. There is nothing you need to be more of. That is the problem. You are more than I can ever be, and I know it."

I tipped my head to the right in confusion. "I meant I should be more professional, but since you brought it up, what the hell, Lars? Look around you. You're the reason I'm surviving in this world. You've handed me everything on a silver platter. Sure, I work for it, but to say I'm more than you can ever be is a bit of a stretch."

He stood there in the darkness and shook his head slowly. The expression he wore was sad, but for the first time, I saw what he was in his soul. He was broken. I didn't know why, but the word filled my head instantly. I smoothed my hand down his cheek and cupped it in mine. "I'm sorry. I don't know what, why, or who, but I know. I'm sorry."

He rested his hand over mine and let a smile lift his lips. "That, right there, is why I know you are more than I can ever be. You see emotions. You understand things the average person misses completely. All I want to do is offer you the same thing, but in a different way."

"I don't understand." I dropped my hand to break the physical contact between us before we started kissing again.

"Let me show you."

He took my hand, and this time, I followed him into the bedroom willingly. I stood next to the bed and waited. He wasn't going to throw me down and have his way with me, unfortunately. He had to pick his mother up soon, so whatever it was he wanted to offer me, it wasn't his body. He opened a dresser drawer and lifted out a box that he carried to the bed. Once it rested on the satin comforter, he motioned for me to open it.

My heart almost stopped at the sight of the black box with the gold insignia K in the center. I stared at the long, slender box before I glanced at him. "Tell me that isn't a fifteen-thousand-dollar vibrator."

He winked but shook his head. "I did not, how do you say it here, fall off a parsnip truck yesterday?"

"Turnip. A turnip truck," I said, chuckling at him.

He pointed at me. "Yes, I did not fall off a turnip truck yesterday. I know you will not use a fifteen-thousand-dollar vibrator, but you must have something better than this." He produced the cheap vibrator from his drawer.

"How did you get that over here?"

"A better question might be, how come you did not know it was missing. Regardless, the time has come for you to open your gift from me."

He lowered the cheap vibrator to the bed to lay next to his box. It was packaged in a hard, unattractive, plastic clamshell. I pointed at the damn pink plastic. "Why do they use scantily clad women on their packaging?"

He raised a brow. "I am not the marketing director here, but I may have the answer to this one. It is a fifteen-dollar vibrator. They are cheap thrills, gag gifts, and discarded after a few uses. You do not have to try hard to sell a fifteen-dollar vibrator."

I tipped my head. "Good point. That said, I could still come up with better packaging than that. It looks sad next to Kontakt's box."

"It is about to be sadder. Time to take the lid off, my little *unerfahrene blauer vogel*."

I dumped my hand on my hip in indignation. "Did you just call me an inexperienced blue bird?"

He smiled just enough to give me the answer. "Sometimes, the truth hurts. No more procrastinating. Take off the lid."

I blew out a breath that ruffled the hair on my forehead and lifted the lid off the box. I took a step back and ran directly into the hard wall of his chest. He wasn't going to let me escape this.

"Now, take it out of the box," he whispered against my ear, his breath hot and his voice low and sensual.

"I don't know if I want to."

"Why not?"

"It's too beautiful. Look at it. I've never seen this one before. Where did it come from?"

"Me."

"It came from you? Like, um …"

He laughed and feathered a kiss across my neck. "While it is close, it is not an exact anatomical replica of me. I designed it and then worked with the engineers to make sure it was exactly what I envisioned."

I noticed the handle then. There was a lotus flower with an S as a stem. Curiosity got the better of me, and I lifted it out of the satin bed. The light purple lotus flower was overlaid on a creamy gold handle. The rest of the vibrator was silicone wrapped metal. A design that could only be described as opulent when you took it in from the side. The glow of the gold in the light of the lamp was enough to tell you the experience was about to be like none you'd ever had.

"This is gorgeous," I finally said after giving it a thorough inspection.

"I call it Serenity."

I whipped around, the vibrator still in my hand. "What?" I asked, my voice loud in the quiet room. "Tell me the engineers don't know you call it that!"

The gleam in his eye told me they did. "If it matters, I had been working on this design for a few months before I hired you. I was stuck on how to make it different from all our other aids. After I met you, I was able to complete it."

"I'm afraid to ask," I muttered, staring down at his chest.

He plucked the aid from my hand and caressed it. A shiver ran through me at the thought of what it would feel like to have his hands caress me in that way. Then I wondered what it would feel like to have him be the one using the device on me. I shuddered again, and the look he gave me told me he knew exactly what I was thinking.

He handed me Serenity and then took the cheap vibrator out of the plastic. He held it up next to his. "What do you notice?"

"The cheap one is straight and pointed. Yours isn't."

His lashes brushed his cheek again when he winked at me, but the moan he made at the same time was new. "Darling, Serenity is yours. It is the only prototype we have. Call her by her name."

I worked hard to swallow so I could speak. "Fine. Serenity is curved, shorter, and tapered at the end compared to that one."

He held it up. "Are you starting to see the difference between a fifteen-dollar vibrator and a priceless one?"

I swallowed around the lump of fear in my throat. "How much did Serenity cost, Lars?"

He shook his head back and forth. "That is unimportant. The first one is always extravagant. We make our investment back when they become part of the catalog. Let me assure you, Serenity will be part of the catalog."

My cheeks flamed hot and red. "Can we not call it Serenity?" I squeaked, and his laughter told me there was no way that was happening.

"Her name is Serenity for a reason. Let me explain." He threw the cheap one on the bed and took Serenity back into his capable hands. He was a creator. A master at designing products to please women, which told me more than I needed to know about what sex with him would be like.

"As you saw at the other shop, all of their vibrators were the same basic design. We do better at Kontakt. I wanted Serenity to stand out but in an understated way. Once I met you, the vision of what our catalog was missing was obvious."

I pursed my lips. "You're saying I stand out because I'm frumpy?"

He laughed then. Full-on sexy, male laughter that made my stomach drop to my toes and my lady parts go instantly wet and tingly. "Frumpy? Seriously?" He lowered a brow and shook his head while his gaze roamed over me, stopping at all the essential places like my breasts, triangle, and thighs. "What I was trying to say was that we did not have an aid for the less experienced woman."

I waved my hand to interrupt him. "You knew the first time you met me that I was a virgin?"

He took a step back. "A virgin?"

I crossed my arms over my chest and hung my head. He didn't know I was a virgin. Fantastic. I managed to tell my boss, the owner of a sex toy company, that the woman he hired is so inexperienced at sex she doesn't know anything about what she's trying to sell.

He tipped my chin up with his finger. "Do not be ashamed, Serenity."

"I'm not," I said, still not making eye contact.

"From where I am standing, you are. I can see it in the way you closed yourself off from me immediately. I did not know you were a virgin. How could I know that upon meeting you the first time?"

"You seemed to know everything else about me," I muttered with a hint of tears in my voice.

He set Serenity back in the box and lifted me by my waist to sit on his bed. I kept my head hanging down, brushing at the nonexistent fuzz on my skirt until he grabbed my wrist. "I may have known public information, but who you are in here," he said, tapping my chest, "can only be shared by you."

I sighed but continued to avoid his gaze. "You said you knew I was less experienced. How did you know then?"

"Call it a gut feeling. The way you reacted to the idea of what Kontakt sold told me you were not comfortable with the subject matter.

You had, what do they say, round deer eyes?"

That brought a smile to my face for a brief moment. "Deer in headlights."

He grinned, and it was adorable, even if I didn't want to admit it. "Yes. Your deer eyes told me you did not have the experience in the arena many other women do. That is not a bad thing, Serenity. I recognize inexperience more readily because of the kind of business I run. I would never disrespect you for your choices as I hope you would not of me."

I glanced up quickly. "Of course not. I'm embarrassed about it," I said shrugging. "I should have had sex by now. Hell, I should have kissed someone sooner than three nights ago." I dropped my head back to my chest. "*Verdammt.*"

He grasped my shoulder and squeezed it once. "There is no timeline for intimacy, Serenity. You can wait as long as you want and for whatever reasons you have. You do not have to explain them to me or anyone else. Please, stop being ashamed when you are here with me. I will not judge you. My chest is bursting to know the kiss we shared was your first."

I swallowed and finally met his gaze full on again. "Seriously?"

His finger trailed down my cheek, and he laid another gentle kiss on my lips. "It has been a long time since I have felt like a teenager, but you make me feel that way. That is why I designed this the way I did."

"You designed Serenity to offer women like me more experience?"

He pointed at me and picked up the cheap one again. "That was part of it, but more I designed her to fit a woman." He held up the cheap vibrator. "This is not shaped like a woman, whereas Kontakt's is. Serenity's length is more realistic, and the shape is made to fit inside you comfortably, adding pleasure in the places a woman needs the stimulation. Feel this," he said, wrapping my hand around the top of Serenity. He hit the plus sign on the handle until the lotus flower lit up. A second push of the button and a slight pulsing massaged my hand. He pushed more buttons and moved my hand up and down, so I was able to discern the differences he spoke of.

"Wow," I sighed, my eyes on the device as he cycled through all the different patterns available. "That's intensely technologic."

He pushed the lotus flower again, and the lights and vibration died off. "I hope you see the potential. If you notice, the pulsing and vibrations are understated and never too intense."

I nodded once. "I did notice that. It was relaxing, yet I could see how it would get the job done."

He tipped his head back to the ceiling and grinned. "I cannot believe the first word you used to describe it was exactly what I wanted when I designed it."

"Relaxing?"

He laid it back in the box. "Yes, relaxing. My goal was to build an aid that a woman of any experience level would find relaxing. While the less experienced woman needs more time to build up to more intense stimulation, a more experienced woman could use it to relax in the tub at the end of a long day."

"It's waterproof?" I asked, staring at it in the box.

"You already know that all Kontakt aids are waterproof. Serenity is no different."

"This might be what you call a game-changer if you can make it affordable to the," I motioned around, "less experienced woman. They'll be younger and not have as much disposable income as someone in their thirties."

He lifted one brow and held my gaze. "You are absolutely right, and that is where you come in. Your assignment is to use Serenity over the next few months and tell me what you like about it, what you do not like about it, and what you think a good price point would be on it. I will leave the researching up to you on how you will arrive at that number."

I swallowed hard, and my face flamed red hot again. "I have to use it?"

He snorted with laughter, and soon, his shoulders were shaking. He stood in front of me, his fingers at his lips and his eyes watering. I smacked him in the arm and he gathered himself, but he couldn't wipe the smile off his face. "Beautiful girl, what do you think it is for? To look at? While Serenity is beautiful, she is not as beautiful as you are. She has a purpose, and you should stop being embarrassed by it. Embrace it. I can promise you that self-pleasuring is one of the best ways to learn about what you like before you get into bed with someone else. Trust me on this. No matter what anyone else has told you, using Serenity will not make hair grow on your palms or strike you blind."

It was my turn to snort with laughter, and I shook my head at him. "Geez, I've had an orgasm before, Lars. I'm not that innocent." I rolled my eyes to the ceiling. When I registered his moan, I slowly dropped my head into my hand. "Sorry," I squeaked, "TMI."

He lifted my chin with his finger again. "No, but all the images in my brain are starting to overpower my common sense. I promise that you have never had an experience like Serenity will provide. There are instructions on how to program the patterns and what buttons to use if you do not want to use presets. The device charges by USB, but it is fully charged now. One charge will run it for four hours."

"Four hours?" I exclaimed. "I'd be dead in four hours."

He burst out laughing again and shook his head, putting the lid on the box while he composed himself. "Then you will not have to worry about it dying at the most inopportune time."

"What about that one?" I asked, pointing at the now rather pathetic looking vibrator still on the bed.

He picked it up and placed it back in the clamshell, then handed me both devices. "Your mission, whether you choose to accept it or not, is to use both of these tonight. I want a full spreadsheet presented to *Mutter* tomorrow about the differences between a fifteen-dollar aid and a Kontakt aid. Graphics are optional."

My mouth dropped open slowly, and I stared at him in fascination. "Tonight? Graphics? Your mot—mother?"

He put his arm around my shoulders and led me toward the door. "Speaking of *Mutter*, I need to pick her up at the airport. Will you be all right at home alone, or do you need me to come over once she is settled?"

I didn't answer, but I blinked at him twice while I worked to control my breathing. Hyperventilating in front of him would only serve to prove his point about my inexperience. A spreadsheet for his mother, though? What was I going to do? I was so embarrassed at the thought I couldn't process what he was saying.

"A spreadsheet?" I whispered in a daze. "What do you want on the spreadsheet? I don't know how to make a spreadsheet like that."

He pinned me up against the door and retook my lips. The box was trapped between us, or he would have plastered his entire body the length of me. His tongue roved at the same speed as his hands, and I didn't know if I was coming or going. I was sure I was much closer to coming. I wanted to, but I didn't want to without him. God, why am I like this? He slowed the kiss down and stroked my tongue languidly twice more before he let his lips fall away from mine.

"I do not want a spreadsheet, Serenity," he hissed. "I do not care if you throw away the cheap one, but you will use the one I created for you, are we clear?" I nodded my head robotically. "I was kidding about *Mutter*, but you and I will discuss what you liked about Serenity and what needs to be improved. Are we clear?" I nodded again. "Good. I do have to pick her up at the airport, but when I return, I will be taking The Diamondback out of my private collection. While I use it, I will be thinking about you at the other end of the hallway using something I designed to bring you pleasure. I know for a fact I will not need the app tonight."

I swallowed, my throat dry, but determination filling my bones. "Feels like you're already halfway there," I said, my tone smart aleck with a side of sexy.

He ground himself against my thigh and laid his lips next to my ear. A hiss escaped them, and a shiver ran through me. "I need a cold shower. Get out of my apartment before I do something I should not, like take your virginity up against this door."

The determination dissipated, leaving my bones like Jell-O. I retreated to the hallway, knowing I wasn't nearly as much of a badass as I thought. "Good—goodnight," I stammered. "Thanks for—uh," I held up Serenity, "this."

He leaned against the doorjamb, his suit pants doing nothing to hide his desires. "It was my pleasure, and now I hope it is your pleasure. Call me if you have any questions. I would be happy to come over and give you a demonstration."

His grin told me he knew exactly what he was doing, and he was going to win, one way or the other.

Ten

Lars

The sky was vibrant with stars and the lights of the city vibrated on the horizon. I stood on my balcony trying to relax, but I could not concentrate on the vision above me with my mind still on the beautiful woman down the hall. The one who had worked her way around my defenses to lodge in the deepest parts of me. She was excellent at testing me and turning me on, the latter being the problem tonight. The whole way to the airport, I had to fight with myself not to turn the car around and take her the way I wanted to up against my door. The only thing that stopped me was knowing she was a virgin.

That was something I could not overlook. Taking a woman's virginity, especially at her age, was too much responsibility for me. It was too much for my immature mind to wrap itself around. I would break her heart and that was not something I could risk. Hell, I was already risking everything. All she had to do was cry sexual harassment, and this company was hers. Sure, she cannot hire the kind of lawyers I can, but I had seen stranger things happen. I did not see Serenity as a threat, though. I should, but I never could get there with it. She did not know anything about running a company like Kontakt. She was a marketing genius, but a ruthless CEO she was not.

"*Mein süßen Sohn, bist du in ordnung?*" *Mutter's* voice filled the balcony, and I lifted my head.

"I am okay, *Mutter*. I thought you were asleep."

She pulled out a chair with perfectly manicured fingers before she sat, her long silk and lace caftan flowing around her perfect size four-figure. Thinking back, I could not picture her ever wearing anything else to bed. I once joked that she was dressed to the nines, day or night. She responded that a lady, a woman who knows her worth, was never dressed to the nines. She was dressed for success, day and night. I was too young to understand what she meant at the time, but over the years, I slowly grasped what she was trying to say. She took pride in her appearance, whether she was in the boardroom, going out on the town, or simply spending time with her family. She was always put together because she was always a lady.

"Hardly. It is after six a.m. at home. The question is, why are you still up? It is almost one a.m."

I shrugged, and she raised one perfectly sculpted brow. In her life, men do not shrug. "It was a long day and I cannot settle."

"Is that not your secret? You are never settled, and that is why you are successful?"

I pulled out a seat and lowered myself to it. I had long ago lost the suit coat and tie. My dress shirt was rolled to the elbows and was obviously hours old. If I was smart, I would go inside, take a shower, and crawl into bed rather than sit here and spar with her. She had slept on the plane. I had been awake for nearly twenty hours. "I would say I am successful because you are my *mutter* and for no other reason. You know how I get this time of year."

"That is the reason I am here. I would never leave you to go through this time alone, but Lars, it is time to move on."

I tipped my head back to the sky and shook it. "You know forgetting is impossible, *Mutter*."

"*Sohn*, I did not say forget. I said, move on. Those are two different things. I know for I had to do it."

"Wash. Rinse. Repeat," I sighed, my eyes trained on the stars.

"What does that mean?" She leaned over the table and folded those long pianist fingers together into a prayer pose. She was ready for battle, and I was ill-equipped at the moment.

"It means we have this conversation every year."

She nodded once. "We do, and every year *geh in ein ohr aus dem anderen*."

I laughed then and lowered my gaze to hers. "No, it goes in one ear and rattles around, it never goes out the other. I do not want to fight with you tonight. I want you to see what I have done here and enjoy our time together, nothing else."

Her eyes, the same blue as mine, sparked with frustration. She never looked a year of her sixty years, and tonight was no different. Most people mistake her for my sister, which is a compliment to both of us. "I only want happiness for you, *Sohn*. You were not happy in Germany, but you also are not happy here."

I leaned forward and took her hands off the table, holding them in mine. "I am happy, *Mutter*. I probably have never been happier than I am in this place. It was exactly what I needed."

"I am not a blind woman, Lars. You look no different than you did when I sent you away. It makes my heart doubly sad."

I patted her hand and leaned back, resting my head on the chair. "It might look that way tonight, but the truth is, in the light of day tomorrow, I think you will see the difference."

She stroked her fine, golden hair for a moment. "Maybe that is the case, and I hope it is. This division is already turning a profit, which means you must be doing something right, at least in business. *Privat?*"

I laughed and shook my head. I expected her to at least beat around the bush a little bit, but then again, she was never one to do that. "My private life is just that."

"Something tells me your demeanor tonight has more to do with a woman than your work. Call it intuition. Have you met someone?"

I was about to walk through fire and I had to be careful or I would get burned, I had no doubt. "I have. You are right, that person is the problem tonight."

"Is she in trouble?"

I tipped my head n confusion. "In trouble? No, why would she be in trouble?"

She tipped her nose down, and her eyes flashed toward her abdomen and then back to mine.

"Oh! God, no!" I exclaimed, holding up both hands. "I just met her."

"That has never stopped you in the past," she pointed out.

"Not this time," I growled, fatigue turning a spark of anger into a flame.

"Then what is it that makes her a problem?"

"Absolutely everything else," I answered honestly. "I care about her, but I am still searching for a workaround to some big obstacles. If I find them, you will be the first to know," I promised, even though I had no intention of telling her first.

She smiled then, relaxed and unforced, but I knew I had not pulled anything over on her. "*Sohn*, it is time you find happiness in both our business and your bed. Jump over those obstacles if you have to, but do not give up because they seem too hard to overcome. I did that once and look at me now."

I leaned forward and rested my forearms on the table. "You did what?"

"I let love slip away, and I have suffered every day since. Now, I am destined to remain in the same place forever."

I rubbed my temple in shock. "I had no idea. I am sorry. Is there any chance you can find him again?"

She patted my hand. "Her." My eyes widened, and she tipped her head at my reaction. "Now you see the obstacles."

I leaned back in my chair as if slapped by an unseen hand. Suddenly, I saw everything through a much clearer viewfinder. "You are a *lesbisch*?"

"I do suppose it was time I told you, but I do not want you to think less of me for it, Lars. I am still your *mutter*, first and foremost."

I shook my head slowly while I forced back tears from my eyes. "Why would I think less of you? You raised me alone as a single woman, and even though it all makes sense now, that does not make your devotion and dedication to me any less. You built a wildly successful business in an industry that was never kind to women, much less a gay woman in Germany. My God, you could not even be openly gay in this business in Germany. I wish I had known."

"Why? Would it have mattered somehow? This is our business."

"It would have mattered, at least when I was older. It would have helped me understand the empire you built if nothing else."

She stared me down and finally nodded once. "I will accept that as my mistake, but I was doing what I thought was right. I had to be careful, so it did not come out about my *privat* life. I was working in a country that did not accept *lesbisch* in the industry. I was protecting all of us."

"I will accept that as a good enough reason, but I am glad to know. I will never say a word to anyone, and when you need to find acceptance, this is the town you will find it in. Here they say, more love, less hate."

She nodded with her lips pursed. "Pulse was a tragedy for the LGBTQ community here and all over the world. It brought back so much fear for us from the past," she admitted, her eyes trained over my shoulder. "That is why I chose Miami. It was my way of, what do they say here? Sticking it to the haters?" I chuckled and nodded once. "A company like this owned by a *lesbisch* and bringing big money into the city. That was important to me, but hate is the reason I remain silent."

I held her hand and sat in silence with her. What she thought about I could not say, but what I thought about was my life from a new perspective. Everything I thought she was had changed with the utterance of a word. "Let me take you there," I whispered after some time had passed. "Let me take you to the memorial. Less hate, more love."

She nodded once, tears gathering in her eyes. "I would like that, yes. We go together as a family."

"Like we always have." I stood and walked around the table, where I leaned down and hugged her around the shoulders. "Like we always have. I love you, *Mutter*."

Eleven

Serenity

I sat on the bed naked and stared into the closet. What do you wear to dinner with your boss and his mother? Or is she also my boss? What do you wear to dinner with your bosses? Especially when they are both the picture of European perfection.

When I met Gretchen this morning, I was immediately taken aback by her beauty. The woman I see on the website every day was someone completely different than the woman I met earlier. She was friendly, loving to everyone she encountered, funny as hell, and ran a hard line on all of it. She laughed and talked business, but she also asked the questions most people in her position wouldn't even think of, much less care what the answer was. She wanted to know everything from everyone. By the time she got to me, she wanted a stiff drink and a relaxing meeting in the garden, which is precisely what she got.

After we drank and got to know each other a little bit, I walked her through the café with Seth. He wasn't his usual exuberant self and barely said three words to any question that was asked. He was nervous. It was evident by the way his hands shook whenever he had to answer a question that was sexual in nature, and the way he continually called her ma'am. I could tell she wanted to throttle him, but her poise was unflappable. She had patted his arm and encouraged him to tell her in his own words what his vision was for the café. With my help, we were able to not only get her approval but her gold seal of approval.

She loved the idea of using the catalog to name the drinks. She even loved the satellite idea for a logo. She said Jodie Foster was her favorite actress. I thought that was a little odd considering she was from Germany, but hey, whatever floats her boat. She liked what we wanted to do, and that meant we could move forward with it. It was another thing added to my already busy workload, but once it was up and running, it would take care of itself.

I sighed and drummed my fingers on my thigh. All they said was dinner. They didn't say where. Casual? Who am I trying to kid? That pair doesn't do casual. They're all fancy, all the time. The clock said I only had a few minutes left to pick something and put it on before they expected me. I grabbed my favorite little black dress and let it slide over my head. It was silky, cool, and hugged me in all the right places. You couldn't go wrong with a little black dress, right?

I grabbed a pair of summer sandals from the closet. The black wedges covered in sequins would add just enough pop. I was glad I had the foresight to get that pedicure the other day. Once in the bathroom, I flicked on the light and gave my hair a once over in the mirror.

"Killing it, Serenity," I said to the mirror, giving the woman reflected back at me the finger guns. "You can handle dinner with two powerful and overbearing Germans any night of the week!"

I burst out laughing and shut the light off just so I could stop seeing my petrified face in the mirror. I was officially losing my mind. I would like to say I got a lot of sleep last night, but I couldn't. I didn't sleep much for multiple reasons. The smallest of which was what Gretchen Jäger was going to think of me. The middle of which was that damned vibrator her son made for me. The biggest of which was her son, his hot kisses and his big … Kontakt.

Since I couldn't do anything about the smallest or the biggest, I focused my attention on the middlest. I threw it in the drawer as soon as I walked in the apartment, took a shower, drank two wine coolers, and paced for ten minutes before I took it back out of the drawer. I stared at it for ten more minutes then put it back in the drawer. He could forget it. No way was I using an aid he had personally designed for me.

As I snuggled into bed, I was convinced something that personal was even more intimate than sex with another person. You don't spend that much time thinking about how perfectly part A was going to fit into part B and not call it intimate. It didn't help that the moment I saw his design, I knew I was going to have to tell him he was right. I hated that those words were going to leave my lips regarding this matter. I hadn't discussed it with him and I didn't plan to, though something told me eventually he wouldn't give me a choice.

I turned the lamp on in the living room, grabbed my clutch, and left the apartment. It was already after nine, and my stomach was grumbling about the lack of food I'd fed it today. I was famished and I prayed dinner was quick and copious.

I knocked on the penthouse door and waited, wondering why I was invited into the inner circle when Seth and Lexie hadn't been. Maybe they planned to make it a working dinner to discuss marketing strategies while we ate. Perhaps they intended to fire me and were buttering me up first. I shook my head and forced the negative thoughts from my mind. *They aren't going to fire you, Serenity. You're their lifeline in the business right now. Without you, they don't have a finger on the pulse of the American woman. Remember that.*

I blew out a breath and nodded once at my inner dialogue when the door opened, and I came face-to-face with Lars. He was all Miami Vice, and the best part was, he didn't even know it. He wore a creamy linen suit with a V-neck t-shirt under it that accentuated his muscular chest. The only thing that set him apart was the classic pair of Melvin & Hamilton leather shoes on his feet. He looked good. No, he looked good enough to eat, and I was starving.

"Hi," he whispered while his eyes took in the length of me, "*du bist schön.*" He shook his head a moment and then sucked in air through his nose. "No, you are more than beautiful. You are unforgettable in the best possible way." He threw me a wink, and I had to work at keeping my knees locked, so I didn't fall to the ground.

"I didn't know what to wear. Thank you for the compliment. I'm glad you like it." I did a small curtesy. He looked behind him for a moment and then grabbed me and planted a kiss on my lips that promised so much more … if only our lives weren't what they were.

"Like is a weak description of what I think about you in that dress. I can barely think with the proper head right now."

My eyes drifted south and paused at the tenting of his linen pants. "Depends on which head is the proper one," I said, flirting in a way I had never flirted before.

What was wrong with me? I swear to God this company had turned me into a horny teenager. Then again, maybe it was this man.

"When it comes to you, I absolutely know which head would like the chance to get to know you. It is the one on my shoulders that tells me we have already crossed the line into workplace sexual misconduct if you so desire to call it that."

"Workplace sexual misconduct? Last time I checked, every time you've kissed me, we've been off the clock, so those three words don't apply here. If I didn't want you to kiss me, I would have already kneed you in the balls."

He snorted, his eyes sparkling with pure pleasure. He pushed me up against the door and braced a hand on each side of me. "While my balls appreciate that, I still struggle with my attraction to you and my need to protect the company. I am not sure I can have both."

That red-headed temper flared to life inside my chest. "I don't want your stupid company, Lars," I ground out, then ducked under his arm. "Where is Gretchen? I'm ready to eat."

"I am as well, *der liebling*. I was famished hours ago." She swept into the room in a dress that could only be described as dazzling and seductive. It was black with a swath of crystals running from her left shoulder, across her breast and down the front of it in a swoop. She had paired it with dangling diamond earrings and three-inch heels.

My mouth fell open slightly. "You're a knockout," I whispered, suddenly feeling frumpy in a dress that made me feel beautiful five minutes ago.

She eyed me up and down and then nodded once. "As are you, *der liebling*." She shook her head. "If I was forty years younger." She clapped her hands twice at her son, who stood behind me. "Is the car ready? We must go."

I followed them to the elevator, my mind wandering to what she meant by that comment. If she was forty years younger? I shook my head to clear it, acutely aware I had better be on my toes tonight, or I was going to get run over by these two steam locomotives on the track. Together they were a team of power, skill, and knowledge the likes of which I had never seen before, and doubted I would ever see again. They knew every little thing about each other and used that knowledge and commonality to their advantage. I didn't have that advantage, so I had to be sure I was always paying attention.

We stepped onto the elevator, and Lars hit the button for the lobby. I noticed his jaw tic, and that told me he was aggravated. *Sometimes the truth hurts, Lars. How pretentious to think everyone wants your company. We're not all out to take what isn't ours.* I thought he knew that about me. "Where are we going to eat?" I asked chipper as ever. "I'm starving."

Gretchen smiled a smile that told me she had something up her sleeve. "It is a private dinner party on the beach outside of 1 Hotel South Beach. All the seafood you can eat and all the mojitos you can drink. It will be divine."

Devine. Well, I was okay with divine as long as there was something besides seafood. "Will there be other food there?" I asked when the elevator left us off in the lobby. The lights were low, but I could see a car waiting for us under the portico. It took me a moment to discern it wasn't Lars' Porsche. It was an Audi A8, four doors, sleek silver, and hot as hell.

Lars held the back door open for me, and before he could close it, Gretchen lowered herself to the backseat as well. Once he was in, he fired up the engine and glanced at us in the rearview mirror. "I am playing chauffeur?"

"You are, *der Sohn*," Gretchen murmured, her smile enough to put one on his face.

He put the car in gear and headed toward the beach while Gretchen turned to face me. "You do not like seafood? You live in Miami."

I nodded and bit my lip. I wanted to avoid eye contact, but her intensity didn't allow for that. If she was speaking to you, she had your eye. "I've never had it, at least not in the last twenty years."

She patted my knee lovingly. "It is time you try it then. Lobster is most decadent when served fresh. Sit by me. I will teach you." Whatever look I wore was enough for her to stop speaking and wait. My eyes flicked to the front of the car, and I noticed Lars was paying equal attention to our conversation.

"What I mean is, I can't eat fish or seafood." I lifted my neck and pointed at a thin scar hidden by my necklace. "When I was four, I tried shrimp for the first and last time. I was in the hospital for a week and went home with a tracheostomy."

The car jerked slightly, and I glanced up to see Lars appear shaken, but he recovered, and the ride smoothed out again. Gretchen opened her purse and pulled out her phone, hitting a number and bringing it to her ear. I started waving my hands when she began speaking, making the cut motion at my neck, and assuring her it was fine, but she never blinked. She spoke to someone at the hotel and informed them there was to be no seafood served. When she hung up, she tucked the phone back in her purse. "Problem solved."

I leaned back against the seat and sighed. "Thank you, but that was unnecessary. Others can eat seafood around me. It's not a big deal."

"I disagree," she said, in her usual CEO tone. "It is a big deal. I will not risk your life by sitting you around a table where seven other people are eating seafood. Steak and chicken will be on the menu instead."

"Okay then, thank you, Gretchen. I'm so used to it that I don't think anything of it anymore. Wait. Seven other people?"

"Yes, *Mutter*. Seven other people?" Lars asked from the front. Apparently, he had found his voice.

"You, me, and five of my closest friends."

Lars groaned, and it turned into a laugh when he signaled and waited for traffic before he pulled into 1 Hotel South Beach.

"Who are your five closest friends?" I asked, glancing between the two of them.

"You will see," Lars said, but that was all he said.

I sat next to Lars and worked to look engaged and comfortable with the conversation. The only consolation I had in my failure was that Lars seemed equally uncomfortable. It turned out that the five closest friends of Gretchen's were adult entertainment talent. I was sitting across the table from General Manhammer, Autumn Lace, Britni Lix, Vance Pecker, and Kurt Hardon. What their real names were, I couldn't tell you since they refused to break character. Don't get me wrong, they were lovely, welcoming, friendly, and engaging, but the subject matter for a girl like me went beyond risqué more often than not.

We discussed the newest trends in the sensual aid industry, which was something I was definitely taking notes on in my mind. As a marketing director, I had to know what was up and coming. Knowledge put me ahead of everyone else when it came to packaging and ad copy.

"We have a new aid that is going to blow the men's market wide open," Gretchen was saying, her voice low and hushed around the patio where we sat on wicker furniture with our drinks in hand. "It incorporates everything a man could want into one device."

General Manhammer leaned forward. "Tell me more."

Lars motioned for me to speak. "I will let Serenity tell you. She named it."

The giant olive-skinned man across from me rubbed his hands together in the evilest of ways. "Oh, the plot thickens."

I rolled my eyes to the starry sky. "It wasn't difficult. The Diamondback is the canister aid for all men. Stylish and sleek, it's everything other strokers aren't. Our patented pulse action provides an even, smooth, sensual experience that is at the very heart of Kontakt's core values. Linked to the app, the sky is the limit to your experience. Unlimited pattern presets are the backdrop to a mind-blowing orgasm. Still not enough? Try the apps selection of adult entertainment, whether homemade or professional. The Diamondback is little but packs a bite you'll never see coming."

General Manhammer stood and clapped slowly. Soon Vance and Kurt joined him while the ladies fell over laughing. Lars sat unaffected, save for the smile tipping his lips ever so much. "Bravo, bravo," the general said. "I've never seen it, and I already want one."

The men sat while Lars passed his phone around with the image of The Diamondback up on the screen. "We'll have some available for testing soon," Gretchen said from her perch next to me. "Who wants one?" All three men's hands went up high and waved back and forth. Gretchen clapped once. "Excellent. As always, it must be kept secret until it is released."

Vance pointed at her and nodded. "Of course. Can we use it in videos once it has been released?"

Gretchen smiled the smile that I was sure got her anything she wanted from any man. "There is no better advertising than word of mouth and honest reviews, is that not correct, Serenity?"

I almost choked on my tongue but recovered and nodded. "That's correct, especially in this business. Anything you can do to spread the word about such an innovative and high-tech aid will help. It will take some time to convince men that The Diamondback is better than all other strokers on the market. Any help you can give us will be appreciated."

"Anything new for the ladies?" Britni asked. She sat across from me in a bikini that was at least two sizes too small while she sipped a Bahama Mama.

I shook my finger at her. "As a matter of fact, we have something in the works." I turned to Lars. "I'll let Lars tell you about it since it was his creation."

The look he gave me would have killed anyone else, but I was made of tougher stuff than what Lars Jäger could dole out. He launched into a description of Serenity, and when he finished, General Manhammer had his lip turned up in distaste.

"Dude, don't quit your day job. You suck at describing your products. That was painful."

I swear I heard Gretchen snort if I thought for a moment that Gretchen Jäger snorted.

Lars huffed in defiance. "I never claimed to be the marketing guru here. I will defer further questions to Serenity since the aid was designed and named after her. She does hold the only prototype of it, after all."

Britni whistled and catcalled. "Let me get this straight. Lars designed a vibrator and then named it after his marketing director. I don't know if that makes him brilliant or dumber than sin."

"Both," Gretchen answered, disdain in her voice when she pinned a look on her son that said it all.

I jumped in immediately to diffuse the situation. "It makes good marketing sense, and he didn't create it after me. He's just mad because I told him to suck my dick earlier tonight. Ignore him."

The table gasped in unison, and everyone proceeded to break out into laughter that lasted much longer than I had intended, which only made Lars angrier. I motioned for them to settle down, and when they were silent again, Gretchen shoulder bumped me proudly. "I knew from the moment I met you *du hast bälle*."

Lars had his teeth clenched together when he spoke. "She does not have balls. That is the problem."

I was relatively sure I was the only one that heard him say it. I hoped anyway, or I was going to have some explaining to do. "Serenity is made for the discerning woman who is looking for a relaxing experience. I would say the technology is much the same as The Diamondback without the app involvement. It's meant for the less experienced user in size while maintaining Kontakt's reputed quality and standards. However, it would be a lovely addition to any woman's collection."

Britni leaned forward. "And what did you think of it, Serenity. Was it everything he promised it would be?"

I froze. What was I supposed to say to that? Do I make something up, or do I answer honestly? Oh God, I was so out of my element here. I glanced between Gretchen and Lars, my eyes wide and sweat breaking out on my upper lip.

"She only learned about its existence today," Gretchen jumped in. "I am sure she will give us a full report once she has had some time to spend on the ins and outs of it." All of their shoulders shook at her remark. I didn't care. She had noticed my discomfort and thrown me a bone, unlike her son. At least someone in the family had some manners and discernment.

Autumn set her empty glass down and motioned toward the hotel. "Who's ready for some bump and grind? There's a fantastic band about to start in the bar."

Gretchen stood. "I have been dying for a Miami mojito. I will not bump and grind, but I will watch you!"

Gretchen had definitely had enough mojitos already, but I wasn't her keeper. Lars stood and folded his hands in front of him. "I am afraid I need to get Serenity home. We both have an early meeting, and it is already late."

"Fine, fine," Gretchen said, looping her arm through Britni's. "Take the car and Serenity. I will bunk here for the night, yes?" she asked the rest of the group who all nodded eagerly.

"We'd love to have you!" Autumn said, clapping wildly.

Lars swallowed, and the look that crossed his face was uncomfortable, but he finally relented. "Of course, *Mutter*. Call me in the morning, and I will send a car for you."

Gretchen waved her hand around. "I will take one of those Yeber's," she said, puffing her chest out with determination.

"Yeber's?" I asked in confusion.

"She means Uber," Lars said out of the corner of his mouth.

"Oh! Uber! No." I shook my head frantically. "Promise me you won't take an Uber in Miami, Gretchen. Not in that outfit."

The General grasped her elbow the way a gentleman would. "I will return her to the plaza myself come morning without a hair out of place. Acceptable?"

Lars nodded once and shook hands with him. We said our goodbyes to everyone else, including Gretchen. He grasped my elbow, not like a gentleman, and led me away from the group without a word. It was going to be a long drive back to Kontakt.

<u>Twelve</u>

Lars

The trip back was quiet, uncomfortable, and absolutely stifling. Serenity sat staring out the window and never said a word as the miles passed. I was biting my tongue to keep from doing one of two things, yelling at her for being that way in front of *Mutter's* friends or begging for her forgiveness. Since I did not want to get into either one in the car, I chose silence in the deafening darkness.

It was the first time I had ever noticed how terrible it could feel to be with someone but still feel alone. I wondered if this was how she used to feel with Babette and Maynard. I wondered if this was how she still felt tonight.

My heart broke at the thought of it. I bit my lip and blinked back the tears that threatened to fall. *Verdammt*! I already knew life was cruel, why was I being like this?

I shook my head and steered the car into the parking lot of Kontakt. The windows were lit sporadically, and behind those windows, some of my engineers were working, others were building our newest innovations, and some lights were on for security. The building never slept, and apparently, neither did I. It had been almost fifteen years since I had slept more than a few hours a night. I guess it was my new normal. I filled those hours at night with business, which was why Kontakt U.S. was already successful after only a few short months. I did not know how much longer I could keep it up, though.

I jammed the gear shift into park, and she glanced at me for a moment, opened her door, and bailed. She was through the doors before I was out of the car, and by the time I reached the vestibule, she was smoke. She must have lucked out and the elevator was waiting for her. The second elevator door opened, and I stepped in, hitting the floor for my office. I would take my personal elevator into my penthouse to avoid seeing her in the hallway. I needed a shower and a shot of brandy before I dealt with her again.

I went directly to the bedroom and stripped my clothes off. The water was hot and exactly what I needed to loosen the tension in my shoulders. There was so much rattling around in my head that I did not know where to start. My gut said to start with her.

After I dressed in a pair of workout pants and a t-shirt, I grabbed a glass and poured a finger of brandy, which I drank standing on the balcony. It took two more shots before I felt the rest of the tension leave my shoulders. I took another shot for the road and then padded down the hallway barefoot. I had to talk to her, even if I was unsure of what to say. I had to make sure there was no disagreement come morning in front of the clients. I would rather have it out with her in the privacy of her apartment than the public boardroom. I probably deserved whatever she had to say, but I hoped she would at least listen to what I had to say, too.

I approached her door and knocked once. I was sure Lexie was long in bed since it was after one a.m., and I forced myself not to call Serenity's name and risk waking her or Seth up. The last thing I wanted them to know was that I visited Serenity this late at night. The door opened a crack, and blackness filled the small opening.

"Not tonight, Lars. I'm tired," she whispered through the hole in the door.

"Me too, but we need to talk about this before morning. I do not want distention in the ranks in front of clients."

"I know how to be professional, Lars. I'm not a child."

"Oh, I am aware. We need to be adults and talk about this."

She sighed heavily, but the door swung open. She motioned me in, dressed in nothing but a towel. I swallowed hard before I stepped in and closed the door behind me. She refused to make eye contact with me and kept her eyes pointed at the floor. "I was in the shower. Let me put some clothes on."

She stepped behind the partition, and it was then that I saw my mistake in the design of the apartments. The barriers were opaque, but when the rest of the space was dark, the light shining behind it gave me more than a PG-rated show. That show left me hard and turned on as hell. I was in big trouble when it came to this woman. She turned the light off in the bedroom and went straight to the kitchen, rummaging around in the fridge.

"Do you want anything to drink?"

"Water would be good, thank you," I answered. I had every intention of holding the cold bottle on my lap until I got a grip on the situation.

The light in the kitchen went off, and she joined me in the living room, handing me the bottle of water. She had a wine cooler in one hand and a shot of something else in the other. She downed the shot and washed it back with the wine cooler. I guess I knew where she stood on the matter as well. She lowered herself to a chair and tucked her leg underneath her. The position gave me a view up her short sleep shorts that even the bottle of cold water couldn't overcome. I grew harder still. She was phenomenal, and I could never have her. It took that thought to finally calm the roaring of my blood.

"It is dark in here."

She lowered the bottle to her leg. "I like it dark sometimes."

"You can hide in the dark."

"Not always a bad thing," she answered, taking another drink of the wine cooler.

I snapped the light on, and the scene came into focus. Her cheeks were red, and her eyes were bloodshot. She refused to look at me, and if she could make herself smaller in the chair, she would disappear. "You were crying."

"Leave it alone, Lars." She tipped the bottle back to her lips and finished it. She disappeared and left me to think about how I was the one to make her cry. I did not have to think hard about why. When she returned, she had another wine cooler. I noticed she drank only pop at the restaurant as though she did not trust herself around alcohol. Now I understood why.

I rubbed my hands on my pants and leaned forward. "I came over to apologize. I am sorry if I upset you."

She tipped the bottle to her lips and drank half of it before she lowered it again. "You have a right to your opinion, Lars."

"True, but it obviously upset you."

She finished the bottle and set it down on the table. "What upset me had everything to do with the fact that you thought I was that person. I'm not. I don't want your business. Besides, I signed your stupid sexual misconduct clause. You're covered, remember?"

My lips thinned at her tone, and I understood that I did not upset her as much as I hurt her, and that hit me straight in the gut. "The clause only applies to the workplace. When we are here or at my penthouse, the clause does not apply."

"Duh, Lars," she said with palpable frustration. "This is our private space. We get to do what we want here without it applying to the business. If you can't separate business and pleasure, then you have a bigger problem."

"This is new for me, Serenity."

She threw her arm out toward her bedroom. "If it's so new, maybe you shouldn't design sensual aids for women you employ!"

A small smile tipped the left side of my lips at her aggravation. "Maybe not, but I did, so …"

"You also should not suggest I give my review of said aid in front of your mother and her five closest adult entertainment friends. That's not me, Lars. That's not me at all."

I leaned back on the couch and nodded, my gaze never leaving hers. "I need to apologize for that, too. I was pissy and it was wrong. I am sorry."

"Apology accepted," she whispered. "I'm sorry for getting angry, even if I had the right to be. I should have been more mature about it. I don't know how to feel, act, or hold my own around you and Gretchen. I get flustered and overreact."

I leaned forward and took her hand. "*Mutter* loves you. Do not worry about her. For some reason, she is a softie where you are concerned."

"I like her a lot, and I don't want to do anything to make her think less of me or that I'm unable to do my job."

I shook my head immediately. "You are doing fine, Serenity. She likes what we are doing here. She told me as much last night."

She tipped her head to the side. "Something was off between you two tonight. I couldn't figure out what it was. Do you not like her friends? You barely said a word other than to throw me under the bus."

"Which you did in return," I said pointedly. "I would have preferred to keep Serenity between us." I pointed to the bedroom and let my hand drop.

She held up her hands. "Truce? I don't want to fight with you, Lars. I don't like confrontation, and I don't like being at odds with the person I have to work closely with."

I patted the spot next to me on the couch. She stood and swung her bottom around to sit next to me. I put my arm around her and held her warm body to me. "Truce. I know we are both stressed right now, and having *Mutter* here only makes it more so. I did not want to start the day out tomorrow still at odds. If I did not say so, thank you for going to dinner with us tonight. I was not aware we were going to have such colorful company, in case you thought I was."

She shook her head. "No, it was easy to see they were Gretchen's friends and not yours. Colorful they were, but they were also sweet and funny. I enjoyed dinner for the most part, even if I was confused about her choice in friends."

I bit my lip to keep from telling her the truth. I could not let on that *Mutter* was a lesbian. As much as I hated to admit it, *Mutter* was right. Staying in the closet was important when running a business such as this one. I would have to do something to distract her, and I had just the thing.

"Did you get a chance to make your spreadsheet on the difference between the two aids?"

She glanced at me out of the corner of her eye. "I'm not making a spreadsheet."

"Paraphrase for me?" I asked instead, hoping she would engage with me about the new aid. "It matters to me what your opinion is about it, Serenity."

She blew out a breath and shrugged out from under my arm. "I need more alcohol if we're going to discuss this."

When she returned from the kitchen, she had two shot glasses of brandy. She handed me one and we clinked them. "*Prost*," we said in unison, which meant cheers in German. We tossed the alcohol back, and it burned all the way down my throat. I set the glass down and leaned back on the arm of the couch, motioning for her to speak.

She blew out a breath, and it rustled the locks around her face. "I needed alcohol to help me say these three words. You were right. The fifteen-dollar vibrator was not better than Serenity."

"Do tell," I said, grinning.

She rolled her eyes but relaxed into the back of the couch. "Not much to tell. I figured Steely Dan's vibrator would surely get the job done. I wasn't going to do anything with them, just to annoy you, but then curiosity took over. You know what they say about curiosity."

"I do," I agreed, smiling.

She motioned to her bedroom. "I found the directions for Steely Dan's and read up on them, then tried it out. The first thing I had to question was why men made vibrators with a point. Comfort was not a word I would use when it came to that thing, but I gritted my teeth out of sheer willpower. I refused to say you were right unless I had no other choice!"

I was working hard not to laugh, but I knew this was not funny to her. I took her hand in mine. "Discomfort is the opposite of what you were supposed to be feeling."

"No kidding," she said with obvious sarcasm. "It gets worse. I turned the base of the vibrator to low as the instructions said, and it nearly jolted my head right into the headboard. Once I unpeeled myself from the ceiling, I admitted defeat. I was going to have to admit it was garbage. I got up and tossed it in the trash can where it cracked open and lay there in all its gutted glory."

"Which is exactly where it belongs," I agreed, throwing her a wink. "At least you tried."

"It was an abysmal attempt. I didn't even want to try Serenity."

"God, please tell me curiosity got the better of you again."

"Not without two stiff drinks and two hours of staring at it while pretending to sleep."

"And when the two hours were up?"

She made the mind-blown motion with her hands. "Never expected what I got. I fell asleep, and this morning when I got up, I used it in the shower."

"Curiosity again?" I asked, one brow raised.

"Absolutely not. I wanted to feel that way again. It was so—"

"Relaxing?" I asked, and she nodded slowly. I did a fist yank and grabbed her chin, planting a kiss directly on her lips. "Best news I have heard all day. Why the indecision in the beginning?" I took her hand and held it to my chest in search of a connection I had only ever found with her. "I worked hard to make sure it would be comfortable and enjoyable for you."

"I didn't want to use it for the reason you just said. You designed it." I went to open my mouth, and she laid her finger against my lips. "Let me finish. I had to face the idea that you designed something to go inside me and offer me pleasure in such an intimate way. Do you understand what I mean? I don't know if there is anything more intimate than that."

"There is, trust me," I whispered, running my fingertip down her cheek.

She shook her head with determination. "Not in my mind, Lars. In my mind, you creating Serenity for me was like making love to me for hours every day. It was like you knew all the little nuances about my anatomy to make it the most comfortable fit possible. It was like all those patterns and settings you made available were ways you would touch me if we were together. Does that even make sense?"

I sat quietly, holding her hand and gazing into her eyes until I could form a sentence again. The effect she had on me always stole my breath and my ability to put together a sensical thought when we were together. "On an intimacy level, it suddenly does, yes. When you separate the act of lovemaking from the emotions, then it makes complete sense. I have to agree with you. I designed Serenity to be exactly like her namesake, soft in all the right places, but hard when needed. You are the tiniest thing I have ever had the pleasure of knowing, and I wanted to incorporate your size into the equation. I wanted to give you a pleasurable stretch without pain. I hope I accomplished all of that."

"And then some," she whispered. "It was scary at first, but then it started to relax me in a way I didn't know was possible. My reaction tells me Serenity will be a solid performer in the catalog once she's in production."

I grasped her chin and brought her lips to mine, where I kissed them softly, leaving them there to linger without making contact until she whined for more. "I cannot tell you how happy it makes me to hear your positive reaction to it. It was my literal wettest dream to know I brought you that kind of pleasure, even if I could not be present."

She grasped my face with her tiny hand and rested her forehead against mine. "You were present in my mind the whole time. You were present on my lips when the pleasure was too much to hold back. You were present from beginning to end."

Seducing Serenity

My lips crushed hers, and I moaned, my body and mind at its limit of the imagery it could handle without touching her. I pressed her against the couch, my hands holding her face in mine while I slid my tongue inside her. I hoped she sensed how much I wanted it to be more than my tongue. She shivered instantly to answer my question.

She did.

She sensed it all.

She embraced it all.

She wrapped her hands around my neck in trust. Her tiny whimpers of need filled the room, and I fought to remind my sex-charged brain that she could change her mind at any time. She could still pull back, but I would take what she would give me right now. I needed a distraction from the images spiraling through my mind of her coming apart from the pleasure I offered her.

She moaned, and I lost myself in her deeper. The thought of hearing that sound in my ear as I slid into her filled me with both pain and pleasure. I ground my already thick erection against her belly until she whimpered under my lips. I ripped mine from hers and rolled off her onto the couch. Our breath was coming in short spurts and I had to swallow before I could speak. "What are we doing here, Serenity?" My tone was filled with desperation and desire, but I did not expect her answer.

"Offering each other pleasure. There is nothing wrong with that, right?"

I trailed my finger down her cheek, and she turned her head, kissing the pad with her lips. "Nothing that I can think of. We are alone, and the dark surrounds us in a way that shuts out the rest of the world. In my business, that is the very definition of intimacy."

She unfolded herself from the couch and took my hand. "Come with me."

"Where are we going?" I asked, standing slowly.

"I'm going to show you how well your design works."

"Show me?"

She nodded, dropped my hand, and walked toward her bedroom. "Show you the very definition of intimacy."

I stared at her receding back in shock. Did she just offer what I think she offered?

My feet moved me forward instantly. If there was one thing that I did not want to miss, it was the very definition of intimacy with Serenity.

Thirteen

Serenity

I think the last shot was one too many. Did I just offer to show Lars how I use his vibrator? Oh my God, what do I do now? *No means no, so turn around and tell him you changed your mind. Easy.* I paused by the bed. Did I change my mind, though?

I spun around and would have fallen over if he hadn't caught me at the last moment. "I don't know what I'm doing, do I?"

He chuckled then and pulled me into his chest, his arms wrapping all the way around me. "If I had to guess, my answer would be no."

"What if I do know, though? Maybe I'm secretly a sex fiend, and I don't know it yet."

His chest rumbled with laughter again. "I think if you were a sex fiend, you would not be a virgin at twenty-four."

"Unless I'm an undiscovered sex fiend?"

"An up and coming talent?"

"Anything is possible. I did use an aid without dying of embarrassment and even took it for a second spin."

"Sounds like a downward spiral into depravity to me."

I smacked him in the chest lightly. "You're making fun of me now."

"No, but I am trying to help you understand I am not pressuring you into doing something you do not want to do."

I gazed up at him from my perch on his chest. "Obviously, since I'm the one who brought it up."

He tapped my nose once. "That does not mean you cannot take it back, which is my point."

"I want to see if the same thing happens again, though."

He lowered a brow at me in confusion. "If the same thing happens?"

My eyes darted toward the bedside drawer. "You know, with Serenity."

"You mean you want to see if you can have an orgasm again? I think your test run this morning gave you that answer."

I bit my lip since I was out of arguments. At least any I could think of while staring into those fathomless blue eyes. "Has anyone ever told you that your eyes are the color of the ocean? But not like the ocean on the shore, but the ocean way out there," I said, motioning with my hand toward the balcony. "The ocean where there is nothing but water and sunshine all around you. They're often stormy, but when I stare into them, they still calm me down."

He kissed my forehead and groaned softly. "I think that was a compliment, but I know you are drunk. Time for bed, Serenity. You will thank me in the morning."

He sat me down on the bed and tried to pull the covers back, but I grasped his hand and pulled him down onto the bed next to me. "I'm not drunk and don't tell me what to do," I whispered, my gaze focused squarely on his soft pink lips.

He took mine with his and laid me back on the bed, one knee between both of mine and his hands buried in my hair. I ground against his knee until he moaned with satisfied desire. I was giving him exactly what he needed, and for the first time in my life, I wasn't afraid. What we had together felt right, and I wasn't scared to show him all the parts of me I kept hidden.

He kissed his way across my jawbone and down into my neck. His lips sucked gently there so as not to leave a mark on my tender skin. I squirmed under him and pushed at his chest until he sat up, the cloud of passion receding from his eyes. Rather than let it stay gone, I grasped the bottom of my tank top and pulled it over my head, letting my breasts out of their trappings for his admiration. I registered the way he sucked in air and slid backward on the bed.

"Serenity." He sighed my name with what I suspected was the reverence Seth spoke of. "I am in awe." His gaze swept across my chest with lust and desire flaring in his eyes. They closed, and he swallowed once. "You are *wunderschönen* in a way I have never known before."

"You think I'm beautiful?" I whisper-asked, scooting closer to him. "My breasts, they're too big for me, I think."

He moaned, and it turned into a half-laugh. "There is no such thing, Serenity. I rescind my statement. You are not just beautiful, you are stunning. I cannot think straight right now."

I trailed my finger up his chest until it flicked up under his chin, where I pushed his mouth closed. "This is only a sneak peek, Lars. There's so much more to me than meets the eye."

He moaned again. "I already know this. Why do you think I designed Serenity after you? I knew how incredible you were the moment I saw you that day at the university. You were the promise of pleasure to come."

I pointed at him and winked. "No pun intended, right?"

I patted the bed on the other side of me, and he took the hint and scooted over. I slid up to the headboard and opened the dresser drawer, thankful the only light on in the apartment was the small lamp in the other room. His breath caught when I took out the velvet bag that held Serenity, a lotus flower on the front the only indication of what was inside. I slid it from the pocket, and he moaned at the slow-motion of it falling into my hand. "She truly is beautiful," I said, holding it up and spinning it left and right.

"I was not thinking *that* Serenity was the beauty," he admitted, his eyes still glued to my chest. I slid down until my head rested on the pillow. He relaxed on his elbow next to me, his warm breath making my nipples pucker when he blew across them.

"You can touch me." I was suddenly self-conscious about his lack of desire to lay a hand on me. His pants were tented, and I worried he was going to pop out of them, so I was unsure why he was holding back.

He groaned and shook his head. "That would not be a good idea. The feel of your skin under my hands would be my undoing, Serenity. I can barely think right now. Touching you will be the end of that."

I handed him Serenity slowly in acceptance of his answer. "I understand, Lars. Would you warm her up for me then?"

Those ocean blue eyes opened to the size of saucers at my request, and he stuttered for a moment. I was witnessing Lars Jäger, the unflappable CEO, entirely out of his element. I had to admit I was enjoying the power I had over him at the moment, though I had no delusions he couldn't take it back at any time.

"Warm her up?" he was finally able to ask.

I grasped the top of the toy and ran my hand down it and back up. "Warm it up. I don't like it cold."

His eyes closed, and when he opened them again, my boy shorts were gone, and I was naked in front of him. The word that fell from his lips told me the effect I had on him was powerful and everything I wanted it to be in the moment. He held my gaze, and the flower on Serenity lit up in a soft purple. I let a seductive smile, at least what I hoped was seductive, slide across my face.

"I do not think you are ready to use this," he murmured against my ear. "You do not have the special lu—

I turned my head and captured his lips, my tongue owning every part of it this time, to prove to him I was more than ready. I grasped his hand and slid it across my belly and down into my red curls. His fingers moved of their own accord, and when he encountered the slickness waiting there, he moaned deeply. "I don't need any help when you're around," I whispered, my lips still on his. "That just happens."

He stole the air from me then, his tongue plunging in to take what it wanted, and his fingers massaging the most center of me with mind-blowing accuracy. I thrust my hips up to meet his hand, and he pushed them back down to the bed gently. Laughter filled his chest while his tongue filled my mouth. Lost in him, I didn't notice what he was doing until it was too late. He caressed my opening with Serenity languidly, his tongue still owning mine. "Lars," I moaned against his lips. "I'm supposed to show you."

"Mmm," he moaned, his body humming with pent up desire. "You are, Serenity. You are. What you are showing me is better than I even imagined when I designed this. I made Serenity as my replacement when I could not be here," he hissed. He held the vibrator against my mound, and I moaned, the sensation still foreign, but equally welcome. "Give me the honor, please?" he begged, and I nodded.

He retook my lips, but this time, he slid Serenity inside me to the rhythm of his tongue against mine. I moaned long and low, fighting against the need to thrust my hips up. The moan ended in a whimper, and he laughed.

Laughed!

I was going to make him pay for that. What he did to me with that toy was the exact opposite of serenity. I was on fire with need for him. Having him so close to me, smelling his cologne, and running my hands over his hard-muscled chest was more than I could take.

"Let me hear how much you like what I made you," he hissed into my ear. "Do you like my version of us, Serenity?"

I nodded, my voice nowhere to be found as he drove me higher on this plane of sensuality and intimacy.

"I cannot hear you, Serenity," he hissed, his tongue dipping inside my ear before his teeth tugged on the lobe. "I asked if you like what I made for you."

"Yes," I moaned, my hips thrusting upward, and he expertly let the toy slide in another half an inch to home plate. "Oh my God," I moaned, "I'm going to come, Lars," I cried, digging my nails into his shoulder. My legs shook with the pure pleasure of his caress, and then I was gone over that edge. My voice rumbled low in my chest when I came loudly with his name on my lips. The pleasure rippled through me even as I floated back to earth slowly. The room was still dark, his breath heavy against my ear, and the toy no longer a part of me. He had me in his arms and was kissing his way from my neck to my ear.

"I have never been so turned on in my life," he whispered, kissing me gently. He didn't linger since my chest was still heaving from the exertion of the orgasm. "That was incredible. You are incredible." His accent was heavy, and his lids were hooded when he gazed at me. "I almost came just watching you. I always knew our aids were excellent, but ..."

I put my finger to his lips to hush him. "It wasn't just the aid, Lars. I didn't orgasm like that last night. That was because you were here. I wanted it to be you."

His lips descended to mine, and what I expected to be a hard, hurried kiss was soft and languid. He sucked my lower lip and bit down for a moment before drawing it through his perfectly white teeth. "I wanted it to be me, too. Tonight, I will go home and use The Diamondback while thinking of you. I won't need the app tonight. I will never forget what I just witnessed."

My hand found its way to the front of his pants and stroked the length of him. "I know The Diamondback is fantastic but is it as fantastic as the real thing?"

"Not even close," he promised, his tongue taking a swipe across my lobe again. "Not even in the same universe."

"Then why wouldn't you thrust inside the real thing? Why wouldn't you want to watch the real thing writhe underneath you?"

"Serenity," he moaned, his hips pressing his hard erection into my thigh. "Stop that talk right now unless you are ready to hand me your virginity on a silver platter. I am so close."

"So close to what, Lars?" I asked seductively.

"Close to coming like a teenage boy with no control."

I wrapped my arms around his neck and pulled him over on top of me, my lips attacking his. When we came up for air, he was all pupil. I wasn't sure he was even breathing. "As far as I'm concerned, I already lost my virginity to you. You're the man I've been waiting for, Lars."

He buried his face in my neck and suckled, his lips surely leaving a mark this time. I didn't care, as long as he was the only one to make it from now until eternity. I ran my hands down his ribs to his butt cheeks, where I squeezed. The longer I massaged him, the louder he moaned into my neck. He thrust against my thigh to relieve whatever pressure was building inside him. "I am losing my willpower, Serenity."

"Good," I whispered, my own tongue swiping across his lobe, "because you have way too many clothes on."

He moaned long and low, the sensation of it coursing through my body. "I do not have any protection."

"I do."

He rose up on his hands and hung over me. "You do? The pill?"

Without breaking eye contact I reached out and pulled the drawer open next to my bed. Inside, condoms were strewn across the bottom. "A gift from the last manufacturer who wanted to be part of the catalog. They glow in the dark."

He thrust against my leg instinctively. "Glow in the dark is unnecessary. You aren't going to see that condom on me before I am inside you."

"Promises, promises," I sighed, toying with his sensibilities.

He raised a brow and then lowered his lips to suck one hardened nipple into his mouth. I gasped loudly into the quiet room, and he laughed again, but this time, it skittered through me like a stone from a slingshot. His hand went to work on the other rosy-red bud, and I thrust upward against him. "Still too many clothes," I cried. My voice was breathy and filled with need again, but this time for him.

He suckled my breast and lifted his head, my nipple still in his mouth until it released with a pop. He didn't speak when he grasped the bottom of his shirt and yanked it over his head. What lay underneath ratcheted up the heat level again until I worried that I would burn all the way through the bed. My hands slid up his chest and through the blond hair that smattered his muscular pecs. "God, Lars," I sighed, "You're beautiful."

He smiled and shook his head. "No, but you are. You are ravishing. I cannot believe I am here with you like this. I have dreamed of it since I first laid eyes on you, but this, you, are even more than I dreamed."

His hands went to the waistband of his pants, and he held my gaze. With deft precision, the pants were gone and he knelt before me in all his muscled glory. I sifted air through my teeth, my desire for him strong enough I could come again without him even touching me. Hesitant, but filled with curiosity, I stroked him, and he bobbed against my palm.

He took my hand in his and closed it around him, showing me how he liked to be stroked. "Do you like how I feel in your hand?"

"I love your velvety softness, but I'll love it more when you're inside me," I said, glancing up at him. His eyes were closed, and he thrust forward at my words, his sanity held together by a thin thread.

Time to cut the thread.

I leaned forward and slid him inside my warm lips, his sharp intake of breath at the unexpected sensation my reward. He grasped my face with his hands and held my head, thrusting gently while I worked him up and down. He moaned in a way that told me he was close to losing it. I didn't want that to happen until he was inside me, call me selfish. I ended the massage and stroked his tip for a moment with my tongue before I leaned back on the pillows. "I'm all yours, Lars."

His eyes opened, and they were filled with lust and passion like I had never seen on another human before. "I hope with my entire being that is true, Serenity." He lowered himself over me and kissed me. His hips thrust instinctively near my opening, but he didn't enter me. My patience was nearing an end, and I grabbed a condom from the drawer while he tortured my breast with his tongue. Slowly he worked his way down my belly to my curls. "I need a taste first," he whispered, his fingers curling around the condom.

His nose nuzzled me, and then his tongue lapped the length of me, slurping and sucking until he had to hold my hips down to continue. My thighs shook from the exertion, and I grasped his hair in my fist. "Stop. God, stop before I come again."

He lapped at me teasingly. "That is the point, my little *Sittenstrolch*."

A sexy laugh erupted from my chest. "Your little sex fiend? Now you're asking for it."

He lifted his head and raised a brow, then tore the condom open and rolled it on, the latex glowing in the night to illuminate his strong erection. "I am asking for it," he whispered, his hand caressing my cheek. "I am asking for it one more time in case you have changed your mind. I do not want any regrets in the morning."

I grasped his glow-in-the-dark cock and directed it back to my triangle. "No regrets. I'm all yours," I promised, poising him at my opening. "Please, take me, Lars."

His hips jerked, but he caught himself at the last moment, entering me slowly, a bit at a time while he watched my face for discomfort. There was none.

"God, you feel incredible," I moaned, wiggling my hips until he had filled me completely.

He settled his pelvis against mine and waited, his head thrown back and his breath heavy in his chest. "It is you who is incredible," he sighed, his hips thrusting once against me. "My chest hurts at how beautiful and right this feels. I had no idea it could be like this. Knowing I am your first is stealing my breath away."

I ran my hand over his chest and left it in the middle to warm him. "Love me, Lars," I begged until his hips started moving again. He lowered his lips to mine, and the change in position changed the way he fit inside me. Already so close to the edge, I lifted my hips to match his thrusts, his demanding but gentle, mine wild and desperate.

"Oh God, Serenity," he moaned. He stilled inside me, buried so deeply I had swallowed him completely.

I lifted my hips more, and he settled in deeper yet. "I'm going to come around you," I cried, trying to hold back the waves that started deep within me.

"Let go, baby. I will follow," he promised, his head thrown back.

I stopped fighting the sensations and fell over the edge again, his moans and cries of desire driving me higher. He thrust forward twice, and my name fell from his lips with reverence as he spasmed inside me. That was all I needed to hear. I no longer questioned if what we had together was forever.

Fourteen

Lars

I glanced at Serenity for the hundredth time since the meeting started. We were in the future Kontakt Café discussing food and beverage options with our vendors. We needed a plan to get it up and running as fast as possible. Did I have to be involved in such a benign aspect of the business? Absolutely not, but I wanted to see Serenity.

    After last night, all I wanted to do was be with her. Every part of her. All of her. Open to me the way she was last night. I had not stopped thinking about the honor she gave me by allowing me to be the first man to make her his. She gave me that piece of her soul. A piece she had held onto for twenty-four years. Now I had to decide what I was going to do with it.

Every part of me but one wanted to stay buried in her forever. It was the part of me that saw the dates on the calendar that reminded me why I could not. I would break her heart in the end, but if I taught her how to love herself and be the sexual woman that I knew she was, she would still thank me. I hoped. I prayed.

I lowered my gaze to the front of my suit pants, and they were once again tented and tight. The simple thought of how incredible it was to be inside her was enough to make me throb with desire.

After she shared her virginity with me, we fell asleep wrapped up in each other. I woke her every hour after that for a repeat performance. I struggle to say I *took* her virginity, as that word implied she did not give it willingly. What we shared was beautiful, and I could not get enough of her. If she thought that box of twelve condoms was going to last, she was wrong. I would use what was left tonight without even trying, she was that easy to love.

Her soft, sensual body wrapped perfectly around mine. The way she whispered dirty bits in my ear in German made me harder than I had ever been before. She may not be a sex fiend, but she made a damn good start at being one last night. After lunch, we might have to retire to her apartment for a meeting of the personal kind if this kept up. And by this, I meant me.

"That should do it then," Serenity was saying when I tuned back in. "Mr. Jäger, do you have anything else?"

I cleared my throat, and she grinned. She knew exactly what she was doing to me sitting there in that pantsuit with a silky cami being the only thing between me and her creamy breasts. "Not that I can think of at the moment," I answered, my voice breathy until I cleared it again. "Feel free to call us with any questions that come up."

We all shook hands, and I was ridiculously glad we had remained seated while we did it. Standing up was going to be embarrassing at this juncture. They packed their items and prepared to leave, but I held onto Serenity's hand, so she did not stand. "We have a few things to discuss, would you walk them out and come back?" I asked, nodding at the man and woman standing by the table.

She cocked her head to the side before she answered. "Sure, be right back."

Seamlessly, she motioned for them to go ahead of her while she chatted them up about the weather and what I assumed was the local baseball team. She was incredibly good at what she did, and she knew it. She more than earned her salary, and I had better be careful not to break her heart too quickly or I might lose her.

"Everything okay? We don't have any other meetings planned for today," she said, coming back into the café. "We scheduled ourselves out to discuss new ideas with Gretchen."

I chuckled and grasped her hand, lowering it to my lap. "Everything is fine, except I was so hard I could not stand up and look professional."

"That is quite the state," she agreed, giving me a subtle stroke since we were still in front of the windows. "I might have a cure for that. Follow me," she said, dropping her hand.

She pushed through the swinging door of the empty kitchen. It was dark, with only a bit of filtered light coming in from the front through the window. She reached behind her and took my hand, guiding me to the back where we kept the dry goods and paper supplies. She yanked me in between the shelving, then her arms wrapped around my neck and she kissed me hard. I moaned the moment our lips met. I fought back with my tongue until I controlled her, nipping, biting, and sucking until she whimpered.

My hand slipped inside her cami to caress her soft breast, the flesh warm and tender under my fingers where I massaged her. She moaned loudly when I ground my hardness against her leg, so I bit her lip gently until she hushed.

"We do not want Seth to find us in a compromising position, now do we?" I asked into her ear, ending the question with a puff of air. She did a full-body shiver and shook her head. "I assume there are no cameras back here?"

"No." It ended on a moan when I slipped my hand down the front of her skirt only to discover she wore no panties.

"Serenity, you are a surprise." I hissed when my fingers parted her folds and found her hot and wet. "Have you ever had a quickie in a storage room before?" I asked, turning her back to me.

"It's always been a secret fantasy of mine," she whispered. I bit down on her neck after I pushed her hair aside and left a mark she would need to leave covered for a good long time.

I raised my head to meet her gaze. "Then let me make that fantasy come true." I pulled her bottom tight to my still clothed erection. "You are going to do exactly as I tell you, right?" She nodded slowly, and I wound my hand around to grasp her chin from behind, trailing kisses from her neck to her ear. "In my fantasy, the little skirt stays, but this cami has to go." I pulled it up and over her head then caught her breasts when they fell into my waiting palms. A gentle squeeze had her moaning and right where I wanted her.

"Too bad we don't have serenity down here," she whispered, rubbing her bottom against my pelvis.

I bit down on her earlobe in response. "I thought I proved last night that when I am in the room, you will be too full for serenity."

"Prove it," she whispered, egging me on.

I turned her head and kissed her hard, and with enough tongue that she was dripping wet by the time I lowered the zipper on my pants. "Never challenge me, Serenity. I do not back down."

"I'm counting on it. Wait. We don't have any protection."

I was already ripping open the condom packet with my teeth. "I may not have been a boy scout, but I am always prepared."

"You weren't last night."

"Only because I was not planning on getting in your pants last night. Today, I was."

I rolled the rubber on and held her belly. "Bend over and brace your hands on the shelf. Remember, we have to stay quiet."

She bent over, and her skirt pulled up over her ass in the most delicious sight I had ever seen. "Like this?"

I grabbed her and kissed her at the same time I entered her from behind, remembering to push forward slowly, so I did not hurt her. She cried out, as expected, but I trapped the sound in my mouth and held her there until she was squirming against me. I wrapped my hands around her breasts and thrust into her a few times. I soon found the rhythm and position that worked the best until she was moaning softly into the quiet room.

"I'm still swollen from last night, and it feels so good," she whispered, trying to stand up straight, but I pressed down gently on her back.

"Stay down," I ordered, quickening my pace, my hands grasping her waist to drive her home against me. "So good does not begin to describe how you feel wrapped around me," I hissed when she pushed back against the shelving. I buried myself inside her, wrapping my arms around her belly and laying over her back. "Your tightness is going to make me come, sweetheart, over and over."

My hips found a slower, gentler pace to stroke her with until both of our legs were shaking, and she was crying my name. I laid kisses across the back of her neck and thrust forward as deep as I could go without hurting her. I sensed the waves, and the moment they stroked my tip, I let go, calling her name and pushing forward, emptying myself inside her until I was weak and panting. She was in no better shape, only upright because I had hold of her belly while her hands hung down to the floor.

"You are okay, baby," I whispered, pulling out and helping her stand. I turned her to me and brushed the hair off her sweaty forehead.

"I'm way better than okay," she whispered, resting her forehead on my chest. "I'm a throbbing mess of sensations, and I think I need a nap."

I laughed softly and pressed my lips to hers for an all too brief kiss. Afterward, I stroked her temple while I gazed into her eyes, hers melted and dreamy. "You blow me away every time, sweetheart. Just when I think you have no more surprises for me to discover, you throw something like that at me. I want to stay lost in you forever."

She pulled her skirt down and straightened it out. "I'd love nothing more, but Gretchen will be waiting for us if we don't get going. The last thing we need is for her to come looking for us."

Her words were like a bucket of cold water dumped on my overheated skin. I reminded myself that the woman waiting upstairs was the reason I could never stay lost in Serenity forever.

Serenity was still glowing by the time we rode the elevator to my office and stepped off. Lexie motioned at the door when we walked by. "She's been waiting for ten minutes. I don't think she's happy."

I snorted with laughter. "*Wird nicht das erste oder das letzte mal sein.*"

"Won't be the first time or the last," I heard Serenity whisper on her way by Lexie. I bit my tongue to keep from laughing. I was full of it today, and it had everything to do with the woman behind me. She walked my walk and talked my talk. If I had half a brain, I would hold onto her. Unfortunately, it was my whole brain that told me what a bad idea that would be. I held the door open to see *Mutter* had situated herself on the small loveseat I had in the corner of the room. Serenity whooshed past me and took her hands.

"I'm happy to see you again, Gretchen. You look rested. Did you have a fun evening?"

Her eyes opened a touch wider, but a smile pulled her lips up out of their frown. "We did have a wonderful time. Britni, Autumn, and I danced the night away. It was delightful."

"I'm so glad you're enjoying your time here. I was hoping we could show you our special vault and then discuss some ideas I had for the catalog. Do you have time?"

Mutter stood and smoothed out her skirt. "But of course, Serenity. I am here for no other purpose. I hope you do not mind that I took the liberty of ordering some lunch. It should arrive in thirty minutes."

Serenity rubbed her tummy and glanced my way. "That should give us just enough time to show you the display room we have for potential clients."

They hooked arms and walked down the hallway, chatting about the dinner last night while I brought up the rear. I felt unneeded, which surprisingly was a feeling I did not mind. I liked that Serenity was able to handle a woman who was challenging to manage at best, and she did it with gusto.

I swiped open the door, since we were the only two with keys, and held the door for them to enter. *Mutter* walked around the room while they discussed what aids were selling best, what aids needed a fresh new look, and how to repackage and design some of our oldest aids to make them modern and improved.

"We have a beautiful dynasty here," *Mutter* proclaimed. "I am in love with this room. It displays what we do at Kontakt in the best possible way."

"It was all Lars," Serenity said immediately. "When he showed me, I agreed it was the perfect way to hook potential distributors." She took Gretchen's arm and walked with her back down the hallway while I locked up. When we arrived back to my office, lunch was waiting, and we sat, each of us opening a box filled with overwhelming scents of deliciousness.

"*Würstchen* from the best little German place down the street. It was nice to see I could get a meal like home in my home away from home."

I swallowed and winked at Serenity. "That was a mouthful, *Mutter*," I chuckled. "Serenity, you were mentioning some new ideas that you had?"

She set her sausage down and nodded, wiping her mouth and lifting a folder from her briefcase. She tapped the folder. "Since you're here, I wanted to discuss with you an idea I had to further the catalog. What I am about to suggest would only be offered in the U.S. catalog to start."

Mutter and I both tipped our heads in confusion, but I spoke. "If it is a good idea, then we should not limit it to only the States. Our company prides itself on being the frontrunner in new technology."

"I agree, but in this case, Gretchen may prefer to keep it here to test the market first." She flipped the folder open and tapped the paper inside. "I want to create a subset of sensual aids made specifically for the LGBTQ community."

Mutter pushed her chair back and stood, her finger pointing angrily in my face. "Two days! You promised not to tell anyone, and yet, you have known for two days, and you already tell people I am *lesbisch*!"

I stood instantly and held my hands out. "*Mutter*, I did not tell her! *Ach du lieber Gott!*"

She sat instantly. "Oh my God is right," she said, her shoulders deflating and her head in her hand, something I never thought I would see in my life.

Serenity sat at the end of the table, her mouth partly open, and her eyes searching mine. *I'm sorry*, she mouthed before she stood and grasped *Mutter's* shoulders in her tiny hands. "I'm sorry, Gretchen. I can assure you, Lars never said anything to me. I have been putting this idea together for quite some time. I meant no disrespect." She closed the folder and tucked it back in her bag. "Let's forget about it and finish our lunch."

She squeezed her one more time and then sat, taking a bite of her sausage. *Mutter* sat up and discreetly wiped her eyes. "I overreacted. I am sorry. I do not do that."

I patted her hand for comfort, knowing she would see anything else as weakness. "It is okay. Life is weird right now. Serenity is nothing if not discreet. You do not have to worry about her outing you."

Serenity swung her head wildly as she chewed. "Absolutely not. As I said, I understand the culture in Germany. I thought since this is Miami, and we have such a large LGBTQ community here, that we could have an extremely successful line if we geared it in that direction. I started working on them the first month I was here. I didn't mean to upset you."

Gretchen nodded and pulled the folder from the briefcase again. "I agree with you, but I was afraid. I am afraid. I worried if I brought it up, someone would find out my secret."

"*Mutter* just told me a few days ago," I explained to Serenity, and her eyes grew as she chewed. "I never knew."

"These are good," *Mutter* said, laying out the pages with computer-generated images on them. "These are really good. These have serious potential."

I stood behind her and eyed the photos while nodding. "Classy and astutely marketed to the right demographics. Made from stainless steel, some of these would be considered high-end to the big names."

I glanced up to get Serenity's feedback. "Serenity?" I asked, staring at her wide-open eyes and the food falling from her lips. "Serenity?" I yelled frantically as I ran to her. I shook her, and she coughed until more food fell out of her mouth.

"Is she choking?" *Mutter* asked, pushing her chair back.

"I do not know! Call an ambulance!" I shouted as the woman I loved passed out in my arms. I did not know what scared me more, the idea that she was out cold, or the idea that I had fallen in love and never saw it coming.

Fifteen

Serenity

I wrapped myself in the darkness of the night and rested my chin on my knees. Miami's skyline was awash with light, and I let my vision go out of focus until the lights blurred into a beautiful patchwork of colors. It had been a long day. I should be in bed, but the drugs they pumped into me to open my airway still had me buzzing. It turned out the restaurant used a fish additive in their sausage, a fish I'm allergic to. I now have epinephrine injectors that I have to carry with me at all times. I'd have to start being more careful. I live in a rough city for a seafood allergy. When I came to in the ambulance, an astute EMT realizing quickly what the problem was, Lars was nowhere to be seen. When I was released from the hospital, it was Gretchen who brought me home.

She had settled me into my apartment and stayed with me for several hours to make sure I was okay. I finally insisted she leave when she couldn't keep her eyes open. We'd talked about a lot of things, but the one thing we didn't talk about was Lars and where he was.

I swiped my cheek on my shoulder to wipe away the tear that fell. I thought after what we'd shared the last twenty-four hours that he would be the one at my side. How wrong I was. The only thing that made my day slightly okay was the way Gretchen had embraced my ideas for the new catalog line. We had talked about it for a long time tonight, but I let her do most of the talking.

I sensed she needed to let it out in a safe environment. She shared her years of heartache over the woman she loved and her shame at having to hide it from her son. I ached for her in places I didn't know I could ache. I let her cry in my arms, something I suspected she would deny if it ever came up. She was the epitome of a lady in this industry owned by men, but secretly, she was just a lonely woman who had come to realize she threw away the best part of her life due to fear and circumstance.

I swiped at my face again and lowered my feet to the floor. I was anxious from the medication they gave me, and I couldn't settle down. It didn't help that I was angry with Lars' lack of concern. I paced into the kitchen to get a drink when there was a knock on the door. It was probably Gretchen checking on me one last time, so I opened the door with a sigh. "I'm okay, Gret—"

The man at the door was definitely not Gretchen. "Hi," he whispered, taking my elbow before I could close the door on him. "Can we talk?"

He moved me into the apartment quickly and closed the door behind him. "Not much to say," I said, hugging myself and walking further into the room. "I was going to bed."

"*Mutter* told me you were okay. I wanted to see for myself."

I shrugged and turned my back, walking to my bedroom. "Your concern overwhelms me."

Before I could lower myself to the bed, he grabbed me around the waist and held me to him, his nostrils flaring as he inhaled the scent of me. "Are you okay?"

I nodded once. "The doctor said it was smart that you got help as fast as you did. It prevented another intubation. I have to carry epinephrine now, which is a small price to pay. I'll be okay."

He lowered me to the bed and knelt, his gaze intense as he stared at me, holding my chin in reverence. "I have been paralyzed with fear for the last eight hours, Serenity. I did not know what to do, and then *Mutter* showed up and chewed me out."

I shook my head sadly. "I didn't tell her to." I scooted back on the bed and lay down on my side, the pillows already elevated the way the doctor suggested.

He stroked my cheek and nodded, the blue in his eyes flat and dull. "Believe me, I know. She was giving me the same lecture she has given me for fifteen years about letting go and moving on."

"Letting go of what, Lars? I don't know what you're talking about."

He sat on the bed next to me and rested his hand on my hip. "Letting go of my brother. My twin brother."

I sat up immediately. "You have a twin brother? Does he live in Germany? Why didn't Gretchen mention him? Where does he work in the company?"

He laid a finger on my lips. "I had a twin brother. His name was Lambrecht. He was my older brother by ten minutes."

I rested my hand on his chest over his heart. "He didn't survive birth?"

He grasped my hand and held it there, his eyes going closed. "He did, and we grew up the way identical twins do. We were always together. When we were fifteen, we were a handful and *Mutter* traveled a lot. My grandfather thought it would be a good idea for us to be in a more disciplined environment." He motioned his hand around. "You call them a school for boys?" I nodded and he continued his story. "We had only been there a few months when one morning, I noticed Lam had not attended breakfast. I went to check on him and he was sick. Sick like I had never seen him, Serenity. I could not save him."

I cupped his cheek and wiped a tear that ran down his cheek. "What was wrong with him?"

He sucked up air and struggled with the next word. It was like saying it aloud made it real, even after all of these years. "Meningitis. Vaccines were not given regularly back then to kids living in dormitories." He paused and took a deep breath. "No one would listen to me and get him help. They said he just had a cold. It was not a cold, and I knew it. I was able to convince them when he spiked a fever, but by then, it was too late. He was gone by the next morning. I was holding his hand when he took his last labored breath."

I wrapped my arms around him, his coming up to hold me desperately. "I'm so sorry, Lars. You did the best you could for him."

He nodded and kissed my neck, leaving his lips there to linger. My anger with him fell away, and I wanted to offer him whatever comfort I could from such a horrible loss. "Tomorrow is the fifteenth anniversary of his death. It is why *Mutter* is here from Germany. She knows she cannot leave me alone this time of year. This year, she has figured out that I am not alone. I have you."

I leaned back and held his gaze. "I never told her anything."

"I know," he whispered, laying his lips on my forehead. "She said she only had to look once to see how much you mean to me. She told me I had to stop being afraid before I was sixty and alone, like her."

I rested my forehead on his. "Gretchen is at a turning point. We talked about it. I can see she's crumbling."

He nodded with his gaze focused on the wall behind me. "I know. I saw it today in my office. *Mutter* never would have done that in the past. It is like she is broken. She is always here for me, but this is one year I am glad I can support her, too."

I brushed the hair off his forehead tenderly. "I'll be here for both of you. I can understand losing someone you love. I lost three before I was sixteen. It's brutal, breath-stealing, and life-defining."

"You did not let it define your life, though."

"I did, just in a different way. I promised myself I would live for them the way they would want me to."

He lowered his forehead to my shoulder and took a shuddering breath. His exhale was heavy on my arm, and his tears wet on my skin. "How come I did not think of that? All of these years, I stopped living because he did. I should have kept living for him."

"Hey," I whispered, lifting his chin to hold his gaze. "It's never too late to start, Lars. Everyone deals with grief in different ways. I can't pretend to know how it feels to live without your other half, someone you are that connected to. You get to grieve any way you want to. No judgments from me."

He smiled and grasped my chin, kissing my lips tenderly. "You never judge anyone, and that is the reason I am here telling you this. When you stopped breathing today, it brought it all back. I was scared with Lam, but today I was petrified. I wasn't sure I could pull air into my lungs as you lay lifeless in my arms."

I grasped him tightly, wrapping my legs around his waist and cuddling into him when he laid back on the bed with me. "I'm sorry. It should have been safe to eat. I'll be more careful, just don't give up on me."

He kissed my cheeks and lips repeatedly. "I should be begging you not to give up on me. I should have been there for you today, baby. I should have been holding your hand, but I was a coward. Will you give me a second chance?"

I brushed my lips across his. "You're here now, that's all that matters. Stay with me tonight."

"Not even that stubborn German across the hall could drag me away," he promised, his lips against my forehead. "Rest now, my little *blauer vogel*. Let me hold you."

My eyes closed from pure exhaustion, but my heart pounded with the knowledge I hadn't screwed up the one thing I needed in this world.

Him.

There was a spring in my step when I got off the elevator. I was filled with news and couldn't wait to tell Lars about it. Sure, there was some trepidation, but I prayed he would be as happy as I was. "Is he in?" I asked, swooshing past Lexie's desk.

"Morning, Serenity. He's in, but listen …"

I didn't listen, I plowed straight ahead and knocked on his door once before I pushed it open. "Lars!" I exclaimed before I was even all the way through the door. I stopped instantly when I noticed he wasn't alone. "Gretchen? When did you get here?" I asked, confused. "I thought you weren't coming back for another month?"

The last month had been ridiculously busy. Gretchen had left three weeks ago, but we had spent hours via Skype late into the night working on the new LGBTQ collection. She never mentioned she was returning early. I glanced back and forth between them and noticed their expression for the first time.

"Close the door please, Serenity," Lars said, his voice low and controlled.

I pushed it closed and set my briefcase on the table. "What's going on? Did something happen?"

Lars nodded once. "You could say that. Do you know what this is?" He handed me an iPad, and I took note of the picture.

"The Diamondback. What's the problem?"

Gretchen stood. "The problem is, the entire project was leaked to a public website known to be frequented by inventors who like to steal other people's inventions. It was uploaded by Lotusflower24."

"As you can see," Lars interjected, "That is our product. We only have one. It is locked in a room down the hallway."

I held up a finger. "Not true, you have one, too. You made sure to describe to me in detail how you use it and that you use my picture when you do." I was angry, and I wasn't going to let him get away with accusing me of something I didn't do.

Gretchen slapped him upside the back of his head and called him a degenerate in German. I had to bite my tongue to keep from laughing.

"Did you upload our most technologically advanced product to a public domain website?" he asked before I could take a breath.

I threw both arms out and shook my head to hold the tears at bay. What they were accusing me of was horrifying. "Absolutely not. Why would I? What could I possibly gain from doing something that would cost this company massive revenue? We have to go on the defense and do damage control here."

Lars pursed his lips. "The information has already been removed. How many people saw it before it was taken down, we cannot say. You and I are the only two people with keys to that room, so tell me what was going through your mind? I cannot believe you would undermine the company this way!"

A wave of dizziness hit me, and I gasped, hanging my head until it passed. "Serenity, are you okay?" Gretchen asked, taking my elbow when I swayed. I shook her away, forcing the dizziness back. My voice was shaking when I spoke. "I can't believe you actually think I did this," I whispered, tears pooling in my eyes. "I don't want anything for this company but success. I don't want anything but happiness for both of you. Doing something like that violates every personal and professional moral I have. It hurts me all the way to my soul to think you would believe for more than a nanosecond that I was responsible for it."

I spun on my heel and ran through the door, down the stairs, and out of the building without looking back.

I held onto Babette's arm and walked with her down the street. "Thanks for taking care of me," I whispered, resting my head on her shoulder for a moment.

"I love you like my own daughter. You never have to question if I'm going to be here for you. It has been three days, are you feeling better about the situation?"

I laughed, and it ended in a sigh. "No, not even a little bit." We walked in silence and I was left to my own thoughts. The situation was complicated and I had no idea what to do about it. When I ran out of his office three days ago, I left behind everything I had in the world other than Babette and the professor. All of my belongings were still at Kontakt, but since I hadn't heard from either Lars or Gretchen in seventy-two hours, I expected said belongings would land on my doorstep soon. If they didn't, I would have to call Lexie or Seth and ask them to get me in when Lars was gone. The last thing I wanted was to run into him while I was running with my tail between my legs.

"There has to be a logical explanation," she said for the hundredth time since I showed up at her door sobbing and hyperventilating.

"I'm sure there is, but that explanation has nothing to do with me. I don't even have pictures of The Diamondback. He's the only one with the design images. I don't get those until we're ready to market it."

"It's all very strange," she agreed.

Pricks of anxiety filled my back, and I glanced behind me, almost tripping when I noticed the car that trailed us as we walked. He pulled up next to us and leaned through the passenger window. "Serenity, I have been looking everywhere for you for days."

"She's not that hard to find when you pull the rug out from under her feet!" Babette called, putting a protective arm around me.

I loved her for her fire and sass, but seeing him again was making me weak in the knees. Sweat broke out on my forehead and I moaned, grasping my belly. The next thing I knew, I was in his strong arms. He lowered me to the passenger seat of the car while Babette held a bottle of water out for me.

"You need to see a doctor," she fretted, even though she already knew the truth.

I pushed the bottle away and shook my head. "I'm okay. It's hot, and seeing him again brought back the horror of his accusations."

"Your eyes rolled back in your head," he said, his tone concerned. "Babette may be right."

"Babette is right," she said, crossing her arms with her usual Louisiana attitude.

I sighed with profound resignation. "A little shade, and I'm already fine. Why are you here, Lars?"

"I need to talk to you."

"The last time you did that, you accused me of what? Trying to ruin you? Trying to steal your company? I don't even know and I don't care. I didn't want your company or your money. I wanted you. You and nothing else." I leaned my head back against the seat. "Forget it."

He knelt and grasped my hand. "I cannot forget it. *Mutter* removed me as acting CEO of the company until I complied with her stipulations."

"Whoa," I breathed out. "What were her stipulations?"

"She told me to get my *scheisse* together."

"It's been three days," I said, shaking my head. "It's taken you three days to get your *scheisse* together?"

"It took me one day to figure out what happened. Another day to sort it all out, and the rest of today to track you down. Please, let me take you back to your apartment. Once you hear me out, I won't stop you if you want to leave."

Babette stood behind him, shaking her head. "Don't trust him, fiy. He doesn't deserve it."

Lars stood slowly and turned to face her, nodding his head. "You are absolutely right, I do not deserve her trust. I broke it once, and by no means does she have to offer it to me again. If it makes you feel any better, Gretchen will be at the penthouse as well. She will not be alone with me. *Mutter* and I both have some apologizing to do. I promise you, she will be free to go at any time, but she needs to move her things if she is going to leave the company. I promise, if you allow me to spend an hour with her, I will bring her back if she so desires."

Babette looked to me, and I nodded. "It's fine," I promised her. "He's right. All of my things are there. Let us give you a ride home, and then I'll call you when this is done."

"I haven't finished my shopping, and the house is only a few blocks away. I'll be fine. I expect a call in one hour." Her gaze was focused on Lars in a way that would have scared me instantly if I didn't know her.

I crossed my heart and blew her a kiss. She caught it and tucked it in her pocket before pointing her finger at Lars. "One hour, or you'll be dealing with the professor."

"Yes, *frau*, you have my assurances."

She stood watching while he closed my door and got in his side, helping me buckle my seatbelt and pulling away from the curb slowly. I waved at her, and she waved back, but the look on her face was one of concern.

"Are you joking about the CEO thing?" I asked, my arms crossed over my chest.

His head swung back and forth. "She was so disappointed in me. Hell, I was disappointed in myself. Things did not go the way she planned."

"She was just as accusatory as you were."

"No, she stated facts without accusing anyone. I was the one who did the accusing. We need to talk about it, but I want to get back to the building. Babette was right. You do not look well."

"I've had a rough couple of days. Is Gretchen really at the penthouse?"

He shook his head again. "No, she is in my office running the company. God, please do not say you are afraid to be alone with me."

I sighed in frustration. "No, I'm not. I don't want to air our problems in front of your mother, that's why I asked. I'd rather we do it in private."

He pulled the Porsche under the portico and motioned for me to stay put. He came around and helped me out, holding me around the waist while we walked in. Seth saw us coming and was holding the door before we got there.

"Are you okay?" he asked, worry creasing his handsome features.

"I'm fine," I promised. "I got too hot outside. I'll be fine once I have some water."

"Please let *Mutter* know we are back and that we will be down to see her in a bit."

Seth punched the button on the elevator. "You got it."

When we reached the penthouse, Lars swiped his key through the door and helped me to the couch. "Let me get you some water." He darted to the kitchen where ice rattled, and water poured from the fridge door. He carried the glass back in and handed it to me. I took a long drink of it and lowered it to my leg.

"Thanks." I didn't make eye contact with him or look anywhere but at my feet. I couldn't, or I would start crying and never stop, I was sure of it.

He knelt in front of me and took my hand. "We know who uploaded the information to the website."

"It wasn't m—"

He put his finger to my lips. "I know it was not you. It took me some time to track it backward. I focused on the idea that the only way to get pictures of the device was to have a key to the room, and it all came into focus. I had never lost track of my keys."

"I always have my keys, Lars. They're always clipped to me."

"I know, which is what was confusing me. Until I remembered the day of your allergic reaction. The EMTs took the keys off your belt. They tossed them on the desk and it was hours until I got back to the office after that. I was up here being a coward with my head in my hands scared to death of losing you."

"You're saying someone stole the keys, took the pictures, and posted them online? Who and why?"

"Lexie, because she was jealous," he said in a breath.

I went to stand but nearly toppled over until he steadied me. "Lexie? There's no way Lexie did this!"

The look on his face told me it was true. "She admitted it yesterday, Serenity. We fired her on the spot and had security stay with her until her belongings were packed. She is gone. We agreed not to press charges, but only because the website admin was able to confirm no one had downloaded the information."

I lowered myself to the couch again, afraid my knees wouldn't hold me up much longer. "Why? What was she jealous of?"

"Us," he answered quietly. "Lexie wanted to be the woman I held every night. The fact it was you made her angry."

"If she got rid of me then she could have you for herself."

He nodded, his lips in a grim line. "It almost worked, too. I almost fell for it until every time I closed my eyes, I saw that look on your face when you ran out of here. I already knew you would not jeopardize the company, but I had to be sure. Everything went so wrong."

"I overreacted, too," I whispered. "I ran to your office because I had exciting news to tell you, but then I saw Gretchen there. Your faces told me something was wrong."

He shook his head and cupped my cheek in his warm palm. "No, you reacted the way anyone would react if they were being accused by the man they love of trying to ruin them."

I laughed softly and looked to the ceiling, so I didn't cry. "How do you know you're the man I love?"

"*Mutter* told me." He winked sheepishly. "She said it was more obvious than the nose on my face."

I rubbed away a tear that had fallen down my cheek. "I told her maybe two or three nights before that how I had fallen in love with you, but I didn't want to tell you and scare you away. You were finally moving on after Lam and I didn't want to put you into a tailspin."

He nodded, biting his lip. "I know, sweetheart. My first mistake was not telling you I loved you that night you came home from the hospital. It was on the tip of my tongue, but I was still afraid. I was afraid of losing you. What I did instead was push you away. I know I do not have the right to ask this of you, but can you ever forgive me?"

My hand caressed his face lovingly. I didn't think I would have the chance to touch him again. To love him again. "I could see how you would think it was me, Lars. I understood that part. What hurt was how you accused me without a second thought."

"Oh, there were hundreds of thoughts that it could not possibly have been you. I lost it, fear overtaking my common sense, and it was easier to push you away than let you hurt me that way."

"You accused me because then you got the control?" He nodded, and I blew out a breath. "I'm sorry you felt that was your best defense against getting hurt again. I should have seen it for what it was, but I was too hurt myself." I grasped his face in my hands and brought him to my lips. "I forgive you, Lars, and I love you."

He sat next to me on the couch and pulled me into his arms. "God, I love you more than I have ever loved anyone before. I have been petrified for three damn days that I screwed up the most important thing in my life forever. Speaking of forever, I want you by my side for it. I want you to be the one to run this company with me, and I want you to be the one who tests all the new products with me." He wiggled his eyebrows and I laughed through my tears. "I promised myself if I found you, and earned your forgiveness, I would not hesitate to tell you all the things I should have said before. Things like I love you, I never want to be without you, and will you marry me?"

He dug in his pocket and pulled out a diamond ring, kneeling on the floor and holding it out. "Serenity Matthews, will you do me the honor of becoming Serenity Jäger? Will you walk with me always, have my babies, and grow old with me? Will you be my wife?"

I fell to my knees in front of him, tears streaming down my face. "Yes," I choked out.

He slid the ring onto my finger and pulled me into a tight hug, his lips near my ear, and his breath warm on my skin. "I love you so much. I have never been more thankful for your forgiving heart." He grasped my face and kissed me like a man who understood he had been given a second chance and was not going to waste it. When the kiss ended, he stared into my eyes, tears in his. "What was your exciting news? You said you were going to tell me something when you came to my office."

I smiled and took his hand, holding it to my belly. The diamond caught the sunlight from the window and threw a rainbow against the wall. It felt like this union had already been blessed at that moment. "I wanted to tell you that you're going to be a daddy. Our love has already been consecrated in the most divine way possible. I love you, Lars."

His breath caught, and the tears fell from his eyes. "A child, already?" His eyes searched mine and I had never seen the blue in his as vibrant as it was at that moment.

"I hope you're as happy as I am."

"I do not know if happy is the word," he whispered, and I swallowed nervously, afraid he wasn't ready to be a father. "Euphoric might begin to describe it. I love you, my sweet *blauer vogel*." He bent and feathered a kiss across my belly and it was then that our hearts beat as one.

Epilogue

Serenity

"Rise and shine, sweetheart," his voice was low in my ear, and his breath hot on my cheek.

"I'm awake and listening for a tiny voice, but all is quiet."

"Maybe we should take advantage of the peace then," he growled, his hands already roaming my bare chest. "I love it when you sleep in the nude."

His tongue and lips worked their way down my neck to my chest, where he captured a nipple in his mouth and teased me mercilessly with pleasure. "God, Lars," I moaned into the quiet room. "You know you're torturing me right now."

He laughed, and it rumbled through my whole being. "You would do the same to me if given half a chance."

Okay, so he was right. In fact, I had multiple times over the last eighteen months. Even when I had to take a break after our baby was born, I had learned how to torture him equally as well with The Diamondback. That aid had gone on to win the new outstanding innovation award of the year in Vegas a few months ago. It was backordered now and would be for months. Good thing we had the very first one tucked away for prosperity.

He kissed his way lower to my curls and dipped his tongue in to taste me. "Sweet as ever," he announced, his hands pushing my legs apart so he could take a longer, deeper drink. My hips bucked, and he lowered them to the bed with his hands while his tongue kept up its practiced striptease. "Are you going to come with me?" he asked, sliding a finger inside me without missing a beat with his tongue.

I moaned at the sensation filling me. "I would go anywhere with you, Lars."

He kissed his way back to my lips and let me taste myself on his tongue. "Come with me to the moon then, baby," he hissed while he buried himself inside me. "I will never get enough of how warm and sweet you are wrapped around me," he hissed into my ear.

I tightened my legs around his waist to draw him closer. "That's because I was created for you and you alone," I promised, lifting my pelvis to meet him thrust for thrust until we were both moaning each other's name into the darkness of the room. He pumped his hips against mine and then stilled, his own orgasm reaching its peak when mine started. His moans were drawn out by the waves of pleasure that buried his seed deep within me.

Sated, all my limbs went slack, and I dropped them to the bed. "I love you, Mr. Jäger, forever," I whispered.

He settled me back under the covers and wrapped a protective arm around me. "I love you, my little *blauer vogel*. Sleep now."

I drifted off with a smile on my face. Lars still used that nickname for me, even though we had a littler *blauer vogel* in the house now.

I woke to the sunshine streaming in the window and a quiet penthouse. I glanced over at the clock and was surprised to see it was already ten a.m. I jumped out of bed and jogged to the nursery, but the crib was empty. There was a note in it with Lars' handwriting. "The babe and I have plans. Text me when you are up."

I laid the note on our bed on my way by and jumped in the shower first. Call me crazy, but when dad has the baby, you always take advantage of it. Once I was out and dried off, I was obedient and texted him. Immediately, a bubble popped up, and a text came through.

Open the closet, you will find a new dress. Put it on and prepare for the best day of your life.

Curious and still naked, I did as he said and found a beautiful white sundress hanging in the closet with new earrings and necklace attached to the hanger. I dressed, adding the accessories and a touch of makeup. I pulled my hair back the way he liked it and clipped it with simple barrettes, then slipped my favorite pair of sandals on my feet. It was warm outside, and I had to be comfortable, especially pushing a stroller.

I texted him then. *I'm ready. Are you coming back soon?*

Your escort is on his way.

My escort? I shook my head and walked through the living room, picking up toys and blankets as I went. Gretchen was here visiting and when she was in town, she rarely left the penthouse, even though she had her own place now. We turned my old apartment into guest quarters for her, but she was only there to sleep. The rest of the time, she was too busy playing with her first grandbaby.

When she arrived last month for the debut of our new LGBTQ collection, she wasn't alone. She brought with her the woman she had longed for all these years. Inspired by the men and women she met here during our work on the new collection, she took a bold step and came out fully to her company. She decided her German counterparts deserved to have access to such a beautiful selection of products. The only way to do that was to stop being afraid. Seeing someone come into their own at sixty was an experience I was so happy to be part of. We had spent the last month getting to know Lina, introducing her to the Miami nightlife, and letting them explore who they could be together after all of these years.

There was a rap on the door and I pulled it open, expecting Lars. I was surprised by the face in front of me. "Maynard? What are you doing here?" I asked, hugging him instantly.

He released me and held his arm out. "It seems I'm supposed to escort you, so let's get on with it, girl."

"Escort me where?" I asked, closing the door of the penthouse behind me. "Where did Lars take the baby?"

"Due time, my child," he tisked.

I glanced down and noticed something on the floor. That's when it hit me. There was a trail leading to the elevator. "Rose petals?"

He helped me onto the elevator, and we rode down to the lobby, me with my hand on my hip and him grinning like the Cheshire cat. "Are we having a family day? Is Babette waiting downstairs?"

"Yes, to both," he promised when the doors slid open and he took my arm, leading me down the hallway to the gardens. There were more rose petals on the floor, and when we pushed through the doors, I gasped in surprise. The gardens had been transformed into a magical wedding venue. The white carpet leading to the gazebo was covered in red rose petals, and waiting at the end of it was the man I had fallen for instantly. He wore a black tuxedo, and tucked in his arms was his mini-me. Our son was wearing a matching suit and my hand went to my chest.

"Oh my gosh, look at Lam," I said, my eyes misting over. At nine-months-old, he was as handsome as his daddy was. The day he came wailing into the world, my whole life changed for the better. He was the spitting image of his father, which meant he was also the image of his uncle, the boy who never got to live. We decided Lam would live on in our family in this way. Now our little Lam kept us laughing every day, something Lars assured me his brother also used to do.

"Those are a couple of good-looking guys up there. Do you want to make them yours?" Maynard asked, holding out a bouquet of red roses to me. I took them from him and brought them to my nose to inhale the scent.

Lars caught my eye and winked while Lam wiggled in his arms. He reached his tiny, chubby hands out and clapped them, making the guests smile at his cuteness. "I'm more than ready. It's time to become who I was always meant to be. Serenity Jäger, the woman who once had nothing but now has everything."

He patted my hand the way a father would. "Can I have the honor of giving you away?"

I smiled a watery smile and leaned into him for a moment. "I truly believe my father was the one who sent you all those years ago to save me. I think he was preparing us for this day. It would be my greatest honor to have you walk me down the aisle."

He wiped away a tear from my cheek, and together, we took the first steps toward my forever.

Seducing Serenity

Protecting Pia

Kontakt Series, Book 2

Seth

I trailed my finger down the plastic numbers on the elevator and pressed one. There was something about the five a.m. hour in this building that I loved. There was something about being able to do my checks and balances without being interrupted every few moments by a phone call or request from another human being. It was peaceful and meditative. It was just me investing tenderness and care into something I loved dearly.

The sleek elevator lowered me from the tenth floor to the first, and I inhaled deeply before I stepped onto the polished marble reception floor of the Kontakt building. Of my building. She was waiting for me to wake her slowly and lovingly the way a man should wake a woman. A soft caress, a gentle nudge, and a lot of coffee. I don't own this building, but this building owns me. She has since the first day I crossed her threshold for an interview. It was three years ago when I applied to be Kontakt's building manager. I didn't even know what Kontakt was, and I didn't care. I needed a job, a place to call my own, and a community of people all working toward the same goal. Kontakt offered me all of those things and more. I would forever be in Lars and Gretchen's debt for the opportunity they gave me.

I caressed the cherry wood reception desk before I clicked on the lamp near my computer. Upstairs, on the penthouse floor, everyone was still snuggled in bed. With living quarters available for a chosen few, I was usually the only one up this early in the day. My boss, Lars, his wife, Serenity, and their son, Lam, reside in the penthouse now. The first time I sat across from Lars and Serenity at my interview, I knew they were perfect for each other. He was a German God for every inch of his six feet. He was older, refined, rich, powerful, and surprisingly vulnerable. Serenity was sweetness for every one of her twenty-seven years. She was younger than Lars, innocent, shy, and powerless but surprisingly, stronger than Lars and I combined. Without her God-given skills in marketing the sensual aids that are Kontakt's business, we wouldn't need this building. She was the only reason Kontakt was successful so early on in the United States.

When Lars moved to Miami from Germany three years ago, he came to open a U.S. division of the company. He would be the CEO, running this division for his mother, Gretchen Jäger. Gretchen was all-powerful in this company, meaning as the owner, she shared the decision making with no one. Since her business was based in Germany, she lived there for the majority of the year. She put her trust in Lars and Serenity to run this side of the business, and in turn, they put their trust in me. I am responsible for the building and its day-to-day operations, and I take my job seriously. Every so often, Gretchen flies over to stay with us. She comes to take care of the necessary business required of her here, but mostly, it's to see her grandson. She flew back to Germany just a few weeks ago but she never stays gone for long. She was always afraid her grandson would forget who she was between visits if she did. Gretchen was vibrant and powerful in a down to earth kind of way. She was ruthless in the boardroom but a loving mother and grandmother the rest of the time. She cared about her employees like family. Our little family was the reason I loved working here. It was the reason Lars and Serenity could be asleep at five a.m. without worry. They instinctively knew the building would be awake and ready when they were.

    When I took this job, I was offered a fully furnished efficiency apartment on the tenth floor. You've never seen someone sign on the dotted line faster than I did for that perk alone. While the apartment was small, it was big enough for a single person who spent most of their day somewhere else. When I wasn't working, I was usually enjoying a beer on my balcony while taking in the lights of Miami. My life was so different from where I was three years ago, even I didn't recognize it. My old life was behind me, and I was never more grateful. Maybe that was why I found such pleasure in the building and the people who surround me now.

I used the high-tech computer app to get the lights on in the hallways and then strolled through the main floor, checking for any that might be burned out. When all of the stairwells were lit, and the gym was up and running, I darted toward the café. Kontakt Café was a full-service coffee bar and sandwich shop. Our baristas would be in shortly, which meant it was my job to get everything ready for them to start serving up caffeine to the perpetually tired.

Once the lights were on, I patted the large etched satellite on the window for good luck before heading back to the elevators. My last job before I retired to my desk for a bit of uninterrupted work time was to check the floors between the first and the tenth to make sure they were ready for the day. I could do the stairs, but today I wasn't feeling it. I decided I'd jump back on the steel cage for a ride to the fourth floor.

Every floor had a specific purpose within the business. Since the second floor was office space for human resources and finance, and the third floor was sales, I could catch those on the way down. It was way too early for any of those paper pushers to be in the office anyway. The fourth floor was engineering, and some of them started their day early, so I always started my floor checks there.

We had in-house engineers who worked on new motors and ergonomic ideas for our sensual aids before they were passed up to the fifth floor to the design team. Once the design team had put together a new prototype, it was handed off to the sixth floor for testing. Once testing had put the aid through its paces, it went to production. Every aid was made in the building and hand-tested before it was shipped out. The ninth floor was reserved for the offices of the CEO and the marketing director. The tenth floor was living quarters. Shipping and receiving were in the bowels of the building and was directed by the good people on the second floor, and myself. If you aren't confused yet, it's a miracle. I needed a cheat sheet for two months just to find my way to the right floor.

I stepped off the elevator on the fourth floor and did my check of the lounge and breakroom. Everything was in order, but I noticed one light burning in an office off the main hallway. It was too early for the lights to be on in all the offices, but it wasn't unusual for an engineer to be having a video conference with someone in Germany. I stuck my head in the door to make sure everything was all right and lifted a brow at the woman behind the desk.

Pia Möller.

Mmmm, she was one hundred percent German goddess. I barely made it through high school, so I had no idea if that was a real thing, but in my mind, she was everything a goddess should be. She was all legs and breasts that left me breathless. Coupled with her bright blue eyes and blonde hair that I wanted to run my fingers through, I could barely form a sentence around her. Her white lab coats did nothing to hide her buxom ways, and her high heels gave her legs for miles. I'd woken up a time or two from dreams of her in my bed, wearing nothing but those heels. She stopped me in my tracks every time she came my way.

When she arrived from Germany shortly after the office opened, she was shy and standoffish. After a few weeks of me bringing her a morning coffee, she lost the attitude and said more than *good morning* and *thank you*. After a few months, she started attending private parties that Lars and Serenity hosted for those of us who live on the tenth floor.

Pia was the whole package and I'd had a schoolboy crush on her since she walked in the door of Kontakt. I wasn't that smart, but I was smart enough to know she was *way* out of my league. She had a doctorate in engineering that spanned multiple different subtypes, from what I'd been told, which is why she was the lead engineer at Kontakt. Lars's intention was to rotate engineers from Germany to train U.S. engineers hired here, but he struggled to find anyone interested or qualified to do the work. When she arrived almost three years ago, she was only supposed to be here for six months. She didn't look to be going home anytime soon. I wasn't complaining. I would enjoy our exchanges for what they were, harmless flirting, but I would never ask her out.

While her goddess features turned me on, her brain scared me, but I still loved spending time with her. She was surprisingly down to earth and easy to talk to. We would share witty banter until she would eventually say something I didn't understand. Not long after that, we'd both walk away uncomfortably. It was those interactions that reminded me she'd never date a guy like me. There was nothing like being embarrassed in front of the woman you had a crush on, and it happened frequently with Pia.

I was stellar at knowing when what I had to offer someone was less than what they deserved. That was definitely the case with Pia. The fact that she lived in the apartment next to mine didn't help matters. I ran into her in the hallway several times a day, which made it all too easy to sit out on the patio and think about what she might be doing behind her own closed doors.

I cleared my throat before I spoke. "Pia? Everything okay?"

She glanced up, and I noticed immediately that it wasn't. I walked further into the room and motioned at her head. "Looks like you have a situation."

She waved the hand not holding a chunk of blonde locks. "No problem, Seth." Her cheeks flushed pink when I stopped in front of her desk.

"It looks like a problem to me. What are you hiding in your hand?" I asked, not making a move to leave.

"I was retesting a prototype the fifth floor insisted had a problem. I did not believe them, but they were right." She let go of what she was holding and a sensual aid swung like a pendulum from her hair. "You do not laugh, Seth Decker."

I held up my hands. "I'm not laughing, but you have found yourself in quite an awkward predicament. How can I help?"

"Would you consider calling Serenity down to help me untangle this? I do not want to cut my hair."

I brushed my hand at her and skirted the desk. "Why bother Serenity when I'm here? I can have you free of your little BDSM mishap in no time."

She huffed at me but refused to make eye contact. "It is not a BDSM mishap. The prototype team insisted the motor had issues and I insisted it did not."

I started unraveling her hair from a small device the size of my pinkie finger. "Who was right?"

"I believe the current picture would answer such question," she snarked and I snickered.

"I believe it does except for the part where you tell me why it's wound up in your hair." I was careful but there were still strands of long blonde hair tangled up in the device as I freed her.

She motioned at her hair. "They said the motor was too strong and would grab clothes and hair. It did not grab clothes…"

"And you decided to try hair. Probably should have found a mannequin for that test." I finally got the device free and handed it to her. "Seth to the rescue."

She took it from my hands and the shiver of desire that skittered through me was dangerous. Extremely dangerous. Pia wasn't the kind of woman to look twice at a guy like me, so falling for her was a surefire way to get a broken heart. That was the last thing I needed.

"Thank you, Seth. I guess it is, what do you say, back to the drawing board?"

I gave her a finger gun. "That's what we say. Maybe it just needs a tweak here or there. It's smaller than most of our devices."

She twisted it left then right. "The motor inside will be used to power several small aids, including a new couple's ring. They put it in this silicone to test it, but I do not understand this. It worked perfectly when I sent it up there."

I sat on the edge of her desk and swung my leg. "Maybe something broke on it when they put the casing around it?"

She tossed it on her desk and rubbed her face. "If that is so then it is garbage and I must begin again. It must withstand great forces considering the aid it was engineered for."

I resisted the urge to pat her shoulder for as long as I could, but eventually, I gave in. Her shoulder was strong but soft and I knew my hand would smell of her sweet perfume all day. "You're the best engineer in two countries. You'll figure it out, but only if you get some sleep."

She brushed her hand at me and leaned back in her desk chair. "Sleep is for the weak. I will sleep when I am dead."

I snorted and shook my head. Germans. They all spoke extremely formal English, never a contraction to fall from their lips, and they were all workaholics. At least until they found someone else to do with their time. Yes, I meant someone and not something. I had seen it happen twice already with Lars and Gretchen. I had no doubt it would happen again with Pia once she returned to Germany.

If she returns to Germany, my subconscious reminded me. I shook my head. She would be going back. Her visa wouldn't last forever.

"Well, Miss Sleep is for the Weak, this guy had better finish his rounds of the building and get back to his desk. The building won't run itself."

"Buildings tend to stand on their own," she said, lifting a brow.

I stood up and pushed my pants legs down evenly. "I didn't say stand. I said run, and this one needs a steady hand at the helm, or all hell breaks loose."

I walked to the door and turned back when she called my name. "Yes, Pia?" I asked, eyeing her as she stood behind the desk again, her beauty making my groin tighten with anticipation. I had to pray I didn't embarrass myself before I got to the elevator.

"Thank you for your help. My hair and I appreciate it."

I patted the doorframe with my hand. "Anytime, Pia. Have a good day."

She sashayed out from behind her desk and I swallowed back the moan that bubbled up in my chest. Those heels were going to be the death of me if I didn't stop staring. "I would like to thank you properly."

I swallowed, wondering what a proper thank you was in Germany. God, let it be a sweet kiss and not bitter beer. "Not necessary. Friends help out friends here at Kontakt."

"That is true, but it gives me a reason to see you again and to, what do you say, chillin?"

I snorted and tipped my head to the side. "Chillax?" She nodded and I grinned. "You need to do that more. You work too much."

"Says many others, too. I would like to chillax with you tonight. Do you know of a good place to chillax?"

I worked hard not to laugh at the way she said the word. It was hilarious but endearing.

"I know quite a few great places. I would love to chillax with you this evening. Should I knock at seven?"

She nodded once in her usual German perfunctory way. "I will look forward to it."

What spurred me forward, I couldn't say, but I placed a kiss on her cheek. "Me too. See you at seven."

I waved, a smile on my face when I walked back down the hallway. There was a spring in my step, and it was put there by a beautiful German goddess on a sunny Friday morning.

Two

Pia

I watched Seth step onto the elevator while I shook my head. "What is wrong with you, Pia?" I whispered aloud. "Check your libido at the door."

I waited until he went off to whatever job was next for him, then I shut down the office lights and locked the door before I summoned an elevator car. It was time for bed after that disastrous night. I normally worked the day shift, but I had a late call with a colleague in Germany. I decided to stay and work on the new motor when we finished. What kind of fool uses their hair to test a product with an already defined problem?

This fool is who.

I stepped onto the elevator and hit the button for the tenth floor, riding in silence. I knew that would not last long. Soon the whole building would be up and at 'em, as they say in the States. I would not be up or at anything. I was going to take a shower and climb into my bed. Apparently, I was going on a date tonight, and I did not want to resemble a zombie. Not when the guy knocking on my door would be Seth Decker.

He is tall, dark, and handsome in every sense of the saying. His hair is dark rich chocolate compared to my honey blonde. His eyes are burnt amber compared to my effervescent blue. His height equals mine when I wear heels, and I enjoy the fact he is slightly taller than me without. It wasn't often that was the case.

I glanced down at the *fuck-me* pumps I wore but could not see them over my *busen*. My breasts were generous by every world's standards and a real pain in my neck, literally. The only thing I liked about them was the look of lust on Seth's face every time he saw me. He was always a gentleman and tried to avert his eyes, but I knew. Every man reacted the same way, but when Seth's eyes lit on them, it never made me feel dirty. He was always respectful.

Working here, I was well aware that desire was not always easy to control. I should know, I had a hard time not throwing myself at Seth every time we passed each other in the hallway. It was completely unprofessional to date a coworker, and as the head of the engineering department, I had to set a good example. That did not mean I had to like it. Somehow, I would have to spin tonight as a working dinner, so no one asked questions I did not want to answer. Most especially should my boss be the one asking them.

Lars Jäger was the nicest guy you would ever meet, but he had his limits. Sure, he dated and married his marketing director when the Miami office first opened, but that was extenuating circumstances. They worked together closely for months as the only two in the building. Besides, they were perfect for each other and denying that would be like denying the giant globes on my chest.

I snorted with laughter when the doors opened, and I came face-to-face with the big boss himself. "Lars," I greeted him, exiting the elevator. "You are up early."

He lifted a brow and let the doors slide shut. "And you are up late. You did not sleep again?"

"*Ende der sitzung,*" I explained and then grimaced. It was difficult to remember to speak English with him when it was our second language. He wanted me to use as little German as possible in the building, though. He worried other employees who did not speak German would perceive it as deceptive. Granted, it was just the two of us in the hallway, but I tried to avoid it all the time, so I did not do it at the wrong time. "I apologize," I sighed, "I am *müde*." I gave myself a cheek slap in frustration. "I am tired."

He laughed and patted my shoulder. "Relax, Pia. You had a late meeting here?"

"No, with Marcus in Germany. I decided to stay and work on a problem we have with a prototype, but I was unsuccessful."

He smiled and tucked his hands into his expensive suit pants pockets. The man was all German god. Serenity was a lucky woman to share his bed.

Good lord, woman. You must need to take a spin with one of your creations because you are, what do they say here? A horny dog?

"Probably because you are *müde*. Get some sleep and try again tomorrow. I am sure you will find a solution. You always do."

"*Ja*," I said, raising a hand in a wave. "Have a good day. I will be in my apartment if problems arise."

"I will let the team know, but I doubt there will be." He glanced around the hallway and took a step closer to me. "*Hast du über mein angebot nachgedacht?*"

I crossed my arms over my chest and sighed. Had I considered his offer? Of course. Had I made a decision? *Nein*. "I struggle with the logistics of it."

"We have options," he assured me. "I want to sit down with you and go over them. Are you free later tonight?"

My eyes darted around the hallway while I came up with an answer. I could not tell Lars the truth now, could I? "I will be available around four p.m. if you are."

"Yes, four is perfect. I will be in my office. I will tell Jada you will be arriving then."

"See you then," I promised.

I swiped my keycard to my apartment and closed the door. Great, now I had a date with destiny and a date with a guy I liked way too much considering he was a co-worker. I pushed off the door and stripped my lab coat off, dropping it on the couch on the way to the bathroom—first, a shower, and sleep. I suspected if I did those two things, it would make the following two items on my list easier to face. I paused by my bed and opened the built-in drawer next to it, removing a satin bag with a drawstring. The pink silicone fell into my hand, and I smiled for the first time all day.

When I stepped onto the ninth floor at exactly 3:58 p.m., my armor was firmly back in place. If I learned one thing early on in my career, it was never to show weakness to a man. Never let them see you cry, yawn, or be flustered. I failed on that earlier today with Seth and Lars. It would not happen again. I would go into this meeting with confidence, even if that was not how I felt. Confidence can hide a lot of insecurity. I had learned that lesson over the years, too.

"Hello, Jada," I addressed Lars's assistant.

I loved Jada. She was young, sweet as could be, and perfect for this business.

"Hi, Pia. How are you?" She came around the desk to hug me, something I rarely got these days. Lars always preached self-love, but sometimes a hug from a friend was what you needed.

I took her hand and smiled. She was the kindest person I had ever known. She had greeted me warmly the first day we met, and we had been friends ever since. "I am well. Always busy, but you know how that is working here."

Jada winked and pointed at the closed office door. "He's a real taskmaster, but I wouldn't work anywhere else. He told me to send you in when you arrived. First, you have to promise we'll do a night out soon. It feels like forever since we had a good old-fashioned laugh fest."

"I agree. Whatever works for you and Serenity will work for me." I tapped my temple. "I need to have some fun. I lose focus when I am stressed out."

"And you're always stressed out. At least you have been recently. I suspect that guy in there is to blame." She raised a brow and dared me to argue with her.

"Not to blame, no. This position is always evolving. I have a lot of responsibility. I signed on for it, so I will deal with it."

Jada patted my back and winked. "You signed on to work here, not carry all of us on your shoulders. We'll aim for next week for a night out." She walked back behind her desk. "And I'm not taking no for an answer."

I held up my hand in a pledge. "I have nothing but my usual work next week. No matter what day you pick, I will be there. I look forward to it." I took a breath in and held it for a moment. "Time to face the music."

"What?" she asked, leaning on the desk. "Are you in trouble?"

I waved my hand instantly in denial. "*Nein*. I was kidding. Going to the boss's office is like going to the principal's office."

She snorted with laughter and shook her head. "I wouldn't worry too much about it. He knows he's screwed without you, so don't take any flak from him, got it?"

I gave her a jaunty salute and headed to the door. I knocked once, and Lars called for me to come in. His office was all masculine lines of dark woods and sleek granite. Lars sat behind his desk with his hands folded against his lips and a smile on his face.

"Good afternoon, Pia. You look much better than you did this morning. I trust that you got some rest. Sit," he said, motioning to the chair in front of his desk.

"I feel much better. Thank you. Sometimes, I lose track of time when I am working alone," I agreed, lowering myself to a leather chair that wrapped around me like a blanket.

"You know that you do not have to work all day every day. Seth tells me you are always in early or here late."

"As though he can talk," I said in response.

He folded his hands and leaned forward on the desk. "This building is his lover. He is always attentive to it no matter the time of day. If you had not noticed, he does not trust her with anyone else."

I quirked my lips and nodded. "I have noticed. I would say it is odd, but I cannot. This building has drawn me in equally as much. The work I do is not important in the overall scheme of humanity, but it is mentally stimulating."

He tipped his head in acknowledgment. "Some might say it is important in the overall health of humanity, though. Sensual aids have been used by many couples to save their marriage. In my opinion, one saved marriage can change mankind. Do not undercut what you do here simply because what you engineer is taboo. You are still an award-winning engineer."

"Who could be working for anyone in the aerospace engineering field. Instead, I had to befriend a guy who manufactures vibrators," I added, tongue in cheek.

Lars and I had been friends forever, and he never questioned why I chose to work for him. He simply knew Kontakt was the best.

He winked and leaned back in his chair. "Maybe you could be, but you said it yourself, this building draws you in and holds you here. At least I hope it holds you here. I want you to stay and continue to lead the U.S. division of engineers. I brought you here because I could not find anyone from the States who had the passion or the drive for the work. I am used to my fellow countrymen who find great satisfaction in creating our aids. That is not the case here."

"It takes a unique person to admit they work for a sensual aid company, as you have learned. It bothers me none to talk about my work, but some, especially Americans, struggle with the idea of talking openly about sex. It has taken me by surprise considering the American culture."

"Astute observation. I noticed the same thing immediately. Most of our employees took a lot of convincing once they found out what we do. There were only a few who had no inhibitions about working here. Seth was one of those few."

I kept my face neutral and forced my voice to stay even. "What you are saying is, you have given up on finding a head engineer for this office."

"What I am saying is, I do not need to find a head engineer if the one I have is willing to stay."

"As my employer, you can tell me to stay for however long you want. Within the legal ramifications of my visa, of course."

He nodded and stood, walking to the window to look out over the parking lot. "I could, according to your contract, but I would never do that. I do not want someone working here because I am forcing them. I only want people here who want to be here."

"I do not have a problem staying, Lars. I am simply concerned that if you rely on me to continue to head this office, when I must return to Germany, you will be without leadership in the most important department of the company."

He spun back toward me and walked to his desk, where he rested his butt. "We have an additional two extensions on your visa to total seven years."

"Yes," I agreed, "your option is to continue to look for someone with hopes of finding them within the next four years."

"Our other option is to enter you in the green card lottery. We would have four attempts before you would be required to return to Germany."

"From what I understand, even that might not be enough."

His leg swung lazily against the desk. "That may be true, but the question is, would you consider trying? I do not want to lose you. Four years is a long time to work out a solution to our problem." He stood and walked back behind his desk. "I would never demand that you stay here. If you want to return to Germany, you may do so. I can hope you want to stay. I would offer you a benefits package to reflect that desire."

I sat for a long time with my gaze fixed on him. He was well-versed in patience and said nothing more while I took my time thinking about his request. "All cards on the table? Is that what they say here?" I finally asked, and he nodded once. "I already have a winning hand in Germany. I am respected, and any company would offer me any benefit to lure me away from Kontakt." He tipped his head in agreement. "The reason I am respected and desirable is because of Kontakt. I have done things with your company that I would never have tried other places, for the simple reason that it was the only way to do it. The Diamondback, for example."

The Diamondback was a male sensual aid that had put Kontakt on the map in the United States. It won a prestigious tech award in Las Vegas and was engineered by yours truly. While most people would be embarrassed to claim a device that helped men masturbate as their crowning jewel, I was not. It was a brilliant piece of engineering that would forever be the feather in my cap.

"You are indispensable here, but I am aware you are sought after by many others."

"I get one offer a day on average. Most never even get opened. I am not looking for a new company. I have stayed here as long as I have for the simple reason that while my hand is a winning hand, it is also a boring hand. Germany is where I lived my entire life. I am not unhappy here learning about a new part of the world. Miami is exciting, warm, and the ocean is my, what do they say here? Happy place?"

He chuckled and pointed at me. "You got it. Miami is different than where we grew up. I am glad you like it here. That gives me hope you may agree to stay."

"There is not much more you can offer me that you have not already offered, Lars. I have a car I do not even drive, an apartment I only sleep in, and more money than I can spend every month."

He shook his finger at me and smiled sheepishly. "Serenity and I have been racking our brains to figure out what else we could offer you. All we have left to offer is property of your own."

"Which I do not want, no offense. I am quite happy living in a place where I am only an elevator ride away from my work. I am used to small and quaint living quarters that are kept up by someone else. I have no desire to spend the time I am not working cleaning a home and keeping up a yard."

His face fell instantly. "That is what I was afraid of."

I leaned forward and tapped his desk. "I do have a proposition that we both could benefit from."

"Anything," he said.

I raised a brow before I spoke. "There is a side project I would like to work on. If you would agree to front the cost of it, and I can make it work, I would give you fifty percent of the profits when I sell it." He was silent, but I could see the look in his eye. I had him. He just had not accepted it yet.

"I am interested in hearing more. However, I do not think you need me to fund this project. I know for a fact that you have plenty of money."

"I do, but if you are funding it, then you have a stake in it. Since I will need to use your equipment, you must have a stake in it."

He nodded once in agreement. "Fine, but I will only agree to recoup my costs. I would not accept the sharing of profits from a sale. I would also require an agreement that you would not leave the company for at least one year after the sale of your creation so as to give me time to replace you. Not that it is possible considering this discussion."

I smiled my gotcha smile and nodded once. "That would not be a problem as I would not be going anywhere. It is strictly a personal project that would be sold to a company far outside anything we do here, in an industry I know nothing about."

He tapped the desk. "*Erzählen sie.*"

I leaned forward and grabbed a piece of paper, preparing a drawing. Do tell, he said, so I took a deep breath and prayed he liked what I had to say.

About the Author

Katie Mettner wears the title of 'the only person to lose her leg after falling down the bunny hill' and loves decorating her prosthetic leg to fit the season. She lives in Northern Wisconsin with her own happily-ever-after and spends the day writing romantic stories with her sweet puppy by her side. Katie has an addiction to coffee and dachshunds and a lessening aversion to Pinterest — now that she's quit trying to make the things she pins.

Other Books by Katie Mettner

Torched
Finding Susan
After Summer Ends
Someone in the Water
The Secrets Between Us
White Sheets & Rosy Cheeks
A Christmas at Gingerbread Falls

Sugar's Dance
Sugar's Song
Sugar's Night
Sugar's Faith
Trusting Trey

Granted Redemption
Autumn Reflections
Winter's Rain
Forever Phoenix

Snow Daze
December Kiss
Noel's Hart
April Melody
Liberty Belle
Wicked Winifred
Nick S. Klaus

Calling Kupid
Me and Mr. IT
The Forgotten Lei

Seducing Serenity

Hiding Rose

Magnificent Love
Magnificent Destiny

Inherited Love
Inherited Light
Inherited Life

October Winds
Ruby Sky

Meatloaf & Mistletoe
Hotcakes & Holly
Jam & Jingle Bells
Apples & Angel Wings
Eggnog & Evergreens
Gumdrops & Garland
Candy Canes & Caroling

Seducing Serenity
Protecting Pia

Cupcake
Tart
Cookie

Butterflies and Hazel Eyes
Honeybees and Sexy Tees

Blazing Hot Nights
Long Past Dawn
Due North

Katie Mettner

His Christmas Star

Going Rogue in Red Rye County

Find all of Katie's Books on Amazon!

Printed in Great Britain
by Amazon